CW01636196

Dead Spark

Dark Magic Enforcer Book 7

To be notified of future release dates, and other news, sign up for the Newsletter at www.alkline.co.uk

Locking Up

"Wake up"! I screamed for the tenth time as I shook Dancer by the shoulders until I swear I heard his brain rattle in his stupid, thick skull.

"Eh? Ugh, what happened?" Dancer ran a hand through disheveled hair, his eyes widening in shock as he brought it down and saw the blood and brains.

"Don't worry, it's not yours."

"Ah, good. Oh, shit!" He shot up off the floor, clearly remembering what we'd both discovered. He tugged at the tattered sleeve of his jacket then ripped it off and rolled up his shirt sleeve. "It's true? We're infected?"

"Yeah, now let's go," I said, already turning for the door.

"But we can't be. It's us. The Head and the best enforcer in the city. This can't happen to us?" Dancer twisted broken skin on his forearm as if he could tear the infection loose and cast it aside. If only.

"Dancer, will you please hurry the hell up? The place is gonna blow any second. We have to get out of here."

He snapped to his senses, finally getting his act together. "Sorry. Okay, let's go."

As magic twisted reality, us stuck in a maelstrom of madness, the fractured wards that kept Council HQ a Hidden sanctuary now wild and dangerous, we ran from his office. We did our best to ignore the bodies we had no choice but to step on to reach the stairs, but it wasn't easy. In fact, it was almost impossible.

Our people. So many dead. But at least the majority had escaped.

We clambered over countless zombies on the stairs, jumped the last section that was missing thanks to the actions of Delilah the dragon shifter, and as colors whirled around us like a demented wizard's idea of a disco, we made it to the door.

All this violence, it was a terrible price to pay. But at least the madness that Dragon had brought to our door was over with, maybe. As I took a final look at the bodies and the spasming interior, I couldn't help but think this was far from the end. Even besides us being infected and the fact we'd soon be a part of an exclusive club—the undead gang.

No way, no bloody way.

"I'm not going out like that," I mumbled.

"Come on, out," ordered Dancer, frantic, and eyes wild. He kept glancing at his forearm and my leg, as if it would all go away and we weren't really bitten by creatures who's virus-ridden saliva was right now coursing through our veins. Corrupting every single cell in our bodies and turning us from men who wielded the most powerful forces in existence into something just as magical but a lot less alive.

This is the problem with this damn Hidden life, there's always someone trying to take what's yours. I just hadn't expected it to be removed in chunks.

It'd been a nice life, for the most part, but I really wanted it to continue. I had Kate, and she had wobbly bits and she let me fondle and lick them, and if that isn't reason enough to carry on living then I don't know what is.

I made a decision right there and then. I'd be damned if I'd be damned. That makes sense, right?

"Oh, for fuck's sake." Dancer yanked my arm while I was lost to my thoughts and the next thing I knew I was standing outside a small, red brick Victorian terraced house.

The door slammed shut behind us.

Dancer bent down and put a key under the mat.

"What the hell are you doing that for? You know we're out of time, right?"

"I know," said Dancer, standing. "But it's symbolic. The end of an era. The end of Dragon. The end of so many of our people. I liked my desk, too."

"I know you did, buddy. I hate to break it to you, but it was one damn ugly lump of wood."

"Hey, I—"

We both felt it at the same time. Energies collided inside the building, distorted magic volatile and utterly wild now. I recalled that the old wizard charged with trying to keep it stable was supposed to be waiting for us but I guess he knew the score and had done a runner.

As the world emptied of sound and reality collapsed in on itself, I shouted, "RUN!" Guess what we did?

Yeah, we ran.

Crouching low, moving fast, we made it about three feet before the world erupted into violence. We were thrown clear across the road from one row of houses to another, coming to a stop as we hit red brick, hard.

I sat up, bruised and hurting on a whole other level, which I hadn't thought possible, and stared back at the empty space where the council once stood. Half the street was gone, nothing but rubble and roof trusses sticking out at strange angles, as if in accusation.

We got up, brushed at the dust—utterly pointless but we have our standards—and marveled at the carnage.

"We'll say there was a gas leak. We have people for this kind of thing," mused Dancer, back in his role as Head.

"Do we also have people for that?" I asked, pointing at the group of wyrmlings running down the street. No, they weren't running away, more's the pity, they were heading toward us, and fast.

"No."

"Didn't think so."

"Run?"

I nodded. "Run."

So we did.

Hi, I'm Faz Pound, and I'm a zombie.

Gimme a Break

"Ugh, no fair," I gasped as my body basically laughed as if to say, "You've got to be joking, dude. You do know what just happened, right?"

I gave it a stern telling off and promised it cake, but it knew I was lying so only partially responded. I switched to threats and swearing as my only backup plan to cajole exhausted muscles into at least trying to move fast.

Dancer sped off ahead and then suddenly stopped at a pillar box at the end of the road.

"Now's not the time to post your mail," I screeched, wondering if he'd lost the plot.

"Quiet," he said as he fumbled with a key and opened a small hatch at the base. He stood, unwrapped a bundle of hessian and smiled an evil grin, all teeth and menace.

"A gun! Are you nuts? We don't do guns, they're dangerous," I warned, the words sounding stupid even as I said them.

It's true, though. We simply do not use them. Partly because they are so scarce, and expensive, but mainly because they're so prone to going wonky on magic users. Same with any device that relies on anything apart from thrusting or swinging.

It's why we stick to magic, and when we can't use magic we stab each other or whack each other with bats. It's the only civilized way to fight, and it stops you getting your hands blown off. Which is always a serious drawback as one preternatural creature or other bears down on you and all you can do is hold up a stump and say, "Um, would you mind not trying to pull my gizzards out, I just had an accident with my gun. Look, no fingers."

"Shut up. Er, please," said Dancer, before he widened his stance, took aim, and did whatever it is you do with a gun to make it fire tiny bits of metal at high velocity, hoping they make a hole in someone you dislike.

It exploded with a noise so loud my ears rang and I was sure that when I turned to look he'd be down one arm and pissed off. But no, the gun was steady and he fired again, hitting a second wyrmling before any of them could react.

Again, and again, then twice more. Then clicks of an empty chamber.

"Tell me you've got more bullets," I said, excited to see the Romanian menaces retreat the way they'd come.

"Nope, that's it. Don't want to push my luck. Anyway, it hardly seems fair to cheat."

"Cheat! They want to kill you, me too, and I bet they don't want to do it in a nice way, either."

Dancer glanced at me quickly. "I thought you said I shouldn't use it?"

"That was before you killed the bad guys. Got any more?"

"No."

"Ah. Um, okay, here they come again. Run?"

Dancer nodded. "Run."

We ran.

Again.

This time we made it a dozen paces before things went awry. A line of five nasty looking dudes came around the corner. We were cut off and out of options.

"Shit," I moaned, just because it was by far the best way to sum up the situation. We skidded to a halt and glanced behind. Yep, they were still coming. At least twenty, so dealing with five seemed like the better option. I sank as deep as I could into the Empty and came up with little more than a slight clouding of the eyes and a fizzle of my ink that died down like sprinklers had been turned on.

I cupped my hands and whispered into Dancer's ear. He nodded and I said, "Ready?" Again, a nod, his hair falling into his eyes before he slicked it back.

"You need to keep a comb handy," I said. Then we sprang into action.

By sprang, I mean we ran at the five men who had clearly expected us to not do something so stupid. As we got close I said, "Three, two, one. Now," and we did the old "kick them in the knackers and then just run away" routine.

It worked pretty well.

For about a heartbeat.

A Gnashing of Teeth

The men either end of the line went down with a satisfying "Oomf" and appropriate screams and moans only those with testicles booted up into their stomachs can manage. We hopped over them like we'd won gold in the newly sanctioned sport of knacker kicking, our victory short-lived as the three with still-dangling scrotums pounced, grabbing us by our already trashed clothes and yanking hard.

While Dancer fought valiantly and I the same, it was clear we would be done for if we didn't get away, and quick-smart. I elbowed, I punched, I kicked, and even did a bit of biting as it seemed to be in vogue at the moment, but I was being bested by a single large lump of a man with a smelly coat trimmed with rancid fur, and a beard that wasn't much better.

Dancer had two to contend with and was faring even worse.

Angry men were closing on us from down the street and just as angry men were punching us and twisting things that should not be twisted.

The only upside was that I wasn't thinking about the bite and the whole zombie thing, but it was little consolation as I got a fist in the side of the head and saw stars.

Then it was silent, and I was free.

I shook, then scrambled to a fighting stance only to find a massive head inches from mine. A gleaming set of razor teeth snapped to the right. I turned to see the face of a man chewed off, and the panther spit out bloody flesh before springing, agile as, er, a panther, at the two attacking Dancer.

The sleek cat raked scythe-like claws down the back of one man, and as he turned it ripped out his throat. Dancer, from his position on the floor, took his chance and jabbed up hard with straight fingers into the Adam's apple of the remaining attacker. As his hands went up, leaving the rest of him exposed, the panther slashed across his belly, slicing through his shirt and deep into flesh.

I pulled Dancer up and we watched, dumbfounded for a moment, before the shouts of approaching wyrmlings made us spring into action. We ran after the already retreating panther, doing our best to catch up but not quite succeeding.

"She's such a fine looking creature," said Dancer, admiring the rear of what I could only assume was

Persimmon and not just a stray that felt like doing a good deed.

"And she saved our asses," I said, not arguing with his observations although it felt somewhat odd to be ogling the gyrating hips of a cat.

We jogged after her, weaving down side-streets, switching back, turning left then right and generally doing whatever we could to lose the wyrmlings.

With breathing heavy, both of us sounding like we had a bad case of "not enough exercise and too much standing around blasting the dark arts"—which I guess was true—we turned a corner and stopped suddenly, neither of us knowing where to look or what to do. Or I felt that way, anyway. Dancer was standing beside me with his jaw slack, wiping at his sweaty brow.

"What, never seen a naked woman in the street before?" asked Persimmon, hands on hips, looking all kinds of luscious. Her body gleamed with a sheen of sweat, her firm breasts high and proud. Waist taut, hips wide, legs you wanted to climb up just to reach the summit and sink your teeth into wobbly bits. Her skin was heaven come to earth. God, I'd forgotten how silky and utterly flawless it was. She was just like her cousin, rich and chocolate, like a mild frothy drink I never know what to call. Glorious, ripe, and entirely distracting.

The only other time I'd seen her naked was when she'd tried to kill me, so this was much better by a long shot.

"Um, no," mumbled Dancer.

"I have. Quite a few, actually. There was the time I was up against the bouncing Blonde from Bo—"

"Shut up, you dick," said Persimmon before she vaulted a wall with some serious skills, proper parkour style, and plucked washing from a rotary line in someone's back garden. She came out the same way she went in, but clothed now in a simple yellow dress.

"Suits you," I said. "Right, Dancer?"

"Eh? Oh, yes. Thanks, Persimmon, you saved us back there."

"No shit, Sherlock."

"She's got a way about her, right?" I said, nudging Dancer. "It's the language, so poetic."

"What the hell is wrong with you?" asked Persimmon, cocking her head to one side.

I instantly felt exposed, so ended up blathering. "Sorry, I think I must have hit my head, along with just about everything else. Okay, we really appreciate the help, but leave it to us now. We've, er, gotta go do some stuff. Important stuff. But, er, not too important. Nothing to worry about."

Persimmon eyed us suspiciously and Dancer didn't help by tugging at his sleeve. I knew I looked guilty as hell, but I crossed my legs to try to hide the exposed flesh of my thigh.

"What are you two hiding?"

"Us? Nothing. You've got a suspicious mind, you know that?" I tried to act casual and only just stopped myself from whistling—that would have been a dead giveaway. Haha.

"Hmm. You sure? I can stick around."

"No, thanks, Persimmon, we appreciate the help, we really do. But please, don't put yourself in danger. I wouldn't want to see you hurt." Dancer mumbled his last sentence. I glanced at him and then understood. He had it bad, real bad.

"Wotcha, Spark," said a cat that sauntered past without a care in the world.

"Oh, hey, Ifstad. How're the kids?"

"Don't get me started, driving me bonkers. Just having a year off. Recharge the batteries and all that."

"Ah, right. Well, see ya."

"Laters, amigo," said the tabby cat that was actually a rather demonic imp Intus had introduced me to a few years ago. He/she/it's nice, but really should try to do a better job of looking like a cat. There was still a slight fork to the tail and the fur looked so matted and mangy you had a hard job to see any face at all.

Ifstad scrambled up onto a wall, pounced onto a shed roof, then disappeared through a window into a house. Probably off to do some important sock hiding work.

"Um, where were we?" I asked.

Persimmon stepped forward, the scent of her strong. Not a perfume, an animal musk that insinuates itself into your mind with promises of sweaty times and strong thighs. I may have gulped, and I know for sure Dancer did. They locked eyes and I'm sure they had a moment. Could she like him? I guess weirder things had happened, but I couldn't for the life of me think what or when it could have been.

This was Dancer, and she was, well, her.

"Let's go," I said, trying to keep my voice calm. Already, the sound of the wyrmlings was getting closer, Romanian dialect, I assumed, and it was angry, and loud.

"Go back over the wall and wait for the coast to be clear," said Dancer, then pointed at the wall like she had never seen one before.

"Now you're acting weird, too," said Persimmon, looking perplexed and staring at each of us in turn like we were hiding sweeties behind our backs and she couldn't have one.

"No we're not, you are," said Dancer, just to make her absolutely positive we were.

"Whatever. Stay safe." And with that she hopped back over and crouched.

With no time to waste, we headed away from the voices. We had thirty seconds before someone found us, if that, so we sped up and ran, again.

Still, it was nice to see Persimmon, and we definitely owed her. Big time.

Fight or Flight

You know when you get in a panic about something and act in ways you normally wouldn't? I think there must have been a bit of that going about as otherwise I wouldn't have done what I did. I mean, a car would have been more convenient, and safer.

As we turned the corner at the end of the street, Dancer mumbling about having to buy a new desk and where was he going to have his meetings now, I yanked him sideways almost off his feet, pulled him into the forecourt of the motorbike store, and ran past rows of sparkling mean machines. I banged the glass door open, hoping to hell that Ethelbald Nazir was in a good mood.

Not likely, he never was. But he owed me and right about now I was sorely in need of a favor in return.

"Ethelbald, where the hell are you?" I shouted, getting panicky and stressed, and maybe a little on the freaking out side, what with the whole being bitten by a zombie thing. Trust me, it has that effect on you.

"Spark, how's it going, buddy?" asked Ethelbald as he came from out back. He wiped a meaty paw he liked to call a hand on his blue overalls and then came around the counter and pumped my hand like a damn car jack.

"Been better, if I'm honest." I shook out my hand, trying to get feeling back. Damn but he was a strong bugger, big, too. He's six feet five, built like a wrestler, has a beard any bird would be happy to nest in, and long hair he seems to keep in a perpetual state of greasy and grimy, making Dancer's look dry and in good condition in comparison. Oh, and don't call him Ethel, he doesn't like it. I did it once, without thinking, and I still have the scar to prove it.

"Spark, we haven't got time for this," moaned Dancer, glancing repeatedly out the floor to ceiling glass window.

"Dancer, or, um..." Ethelbald scratched his head, "is it Head Dancer now?"

"Dancer's fine," he said, distracted.

"Hey, how come you guys never come see me? I'm just around the corner from you."

We stared at him like he'd lost the plot. Surely he'd heard the explosion? Then I realized that with the bikes running in the garage, not to mention the thrash metal playing at full volume, his own business could go up in a nuclear explosion and he'd never hear it. Probably not notice, either.

"Sorry," I mumbled, knowing I really should visit him more often. We go way back, and I hadn't stopped by since before Tokyo.

"So, you're back? Couldn't stay away from the old magic, eh?" he asked, jovially.

"Long story. Look, gotta be quick. Being chased. Need bikes, now. Special ones if you have them."

"Why didn't you say so? Come on. I got two real beauties just finished up. Cost you, though." Ethelbald grabbed keys from a board behind the counter and we followed him out onto the forecourt.

"Bikes?" Dancer looked nervous.

"Yeah, bikes. Got a better idea?"

"A car?"

"Well, the wyrmlings are where the cars are. You wanna fight them? Cause I know I'm about done for and there's no way I can use magic. I need to rest. I'm running on empty."

Dancer checked the street and ran back up to us in a panic. "They're coming. We have to go. Right now."

"Okay, okay. Which bikes? Sorry, I'll come visit soon."

Ethelbald stepped aside and smiled. "Check it out, dudes. These are my best work yet. Full of life and with all the usual upgrades and some new surprises for the discerning client. Here." He handed us a key each and wasting no time I jumped on and Dancer did likewise.

The bikes roared into life, sounding like two demons growling with happiness. I revved the entirely bespoke machine and shouted to Dancer, "How do we stop the you-know-what from turning us?"

"Follow me," he shouted, then burned rubber into the concrete and was out on the road and changing up the gears in a second.

"Be careful with them, they cost a bloody fortune," shouted Ethelbald as I chased after Dancer, burning a matching scorch line of panic-fueled rubber onto the forecourt.

"We'll pay you when we get back," I said optimistically. Gotta stay positive.

I checked the fuel gauge—enough to get us far away—and was surprised to find I was already up to sixty with no sign of the bike struggling.

"Damn, should have got a helmet," I muttered, also realizing it was a bad idea to drive a machine usually reserved for adrenaline junkies in a shredded suit and winklepickers.

Too late now. I turned to see the wyrmlings in the street slowing down, knowing they couldn't catch us.

Facing front, I gave the bike some throttle and tore through the suburbs of Cardiff breaking every rule of the road as I tried to catch up with Dancer.

He better have a good way to deal with this as otherwise we'd be very dead, very soon.

A Moment

As we hurtled through the city, I tried to take stock of my body—it wasn't good. All of me ached, all of me screamed in pain, all of me was dog-tired. Using magic until you reach exhaustion, until you couldn't blast an ant if it was on your nose, it drains you in ways that go beyond merely feeling physically tired. It goes much deeper than that.

Yet, even after what had happened, the fighting and chasing around the city in a constant state of hyped-up alertness, I wasn't hurtling toward a black pit of pain and despair like I used to. I was done for, no question, but there was an inner strength that was a part of me now. The giant within kept me going, strong and indomitable no matter what. I felt this difference like a perpetual reserve—it could never be tapped out. Making me a new man, one that would never again be at the whims of the magical comedown as I had been for so many years.

I was different, new and improved, which meant it was a crying shame I'd been bitten and might not live to see the new me emerge now I'd accepted my link to magic and had decided I could no more give it up than I could stop breathing. There was an inner peace even while my mind and body raged at the chaos we fled from.

Dragon was defeated, many of his followers were dead, and I didn't doubt that given time the wyrmlings would crawl back under the rocks they'd emerged from. But for now, well, they hated us with a vengeance that knew no bounds—undoubtedly, we hadn't seen the last of them.

They'd be after us, wanted retribution for playing our part in destroying the man they idolized, worshiped like a god, and had been waiting for to lead them to glory. Tough. He was insane, and now he was dead. Good riddance.

I glanced down at my leg, the bite mark partially visible where I'd ripped away the material to get a better look. It was kind of a funny color, like when you get a bruise that fades, all purplish and green. This was just the beginning, though. Soon it would change, the bruising spreading, becoming more evident as the virus really took hold and got to work on my flesh and my insides. Changing me, turning me zombie.

I know, right? Eek!

How was Faz Pound supposed to talk about himself in the third person if he was a mindless creature obsessed with nothing more than brains? He was usually obsessed with boobs and magic, and that suited him just fine.

Everything was in turmoil, not just my mind. Where was everyone who'd left before the building exploded? Presumably they'd simply done a runner, which was sensible, but I didn't like not being certain. What about Kate, and Mithnite? Were they all right? And why was I even thinking they weren't? They were at home, safe and sound, but I'd call as soon as I could, just to be sure. The thought made my stomach flip, insides churning at the conversation.

What would I say? "Hi, Kate. Good news, Dragon's dead. His wife ate him. Oh, by the way, I got bitten by a zombie and I can't come home in case I eat you and our new house guest. Love ya. Toodles."

No, best to say nothing, at least until I got a handle on the situation. How, exactly, was another matter, but Dancer had said he had an idea, so maybe there was hope. The one thing we both had going for us was that we were deeply entrenched in all things magic. We could fight it, draw on our power, our connection to the Empty, and stave off the all-encompassing zombieness for a while.

It would have been better if I was full of magic, not running on scant reserves so weak as to be next to meaningless, but Dancer and I had been users, and abusers, of magic for so long we were almost true Hidden. Especially with his age and my newfound abilities. That gave us a level of protection and a way to fight this thing that Regulars, and most Hidden, would never have.

That's not to say I wasn't terrified. I knew for a fact I'd rather be killed than be a zombie. Yes, I know that's being dead, too, but if I was to die it would be permanently, not a walking thing that would slowly rot away caring only about brains, brains, and more brains.

What a life. I come out of magical retirement and this is the thanks I get for saving the bloody world from a madman. Makes you wonder if there's any point, when all you get for your trouble is a hole in your nice suit and an itch spreading from your thigh that makes you want to claw off your own flesh.

The intensity of the tingling and throbbing became utterly maddening, driving me to distraction. I don't know how much of it was the poison spreading—and you can bet I was doing all I could to prevent it from happening, driving as much magic into the wound as I could to stop being consumed—and how much was my mind playing tricks on me.

Glancing down, I almost drove straight into the back of Dancer as I finally caught up with him. We were already out on a clear, fast road now heading away for the city, and that was good. At least the wyrmlings wouldn't catch us and cause mayhem where innocents could be hurt.

I pulled alongside Dancer and shouted, "Where to?" but before he answered, my bike kicked and I was thrown forward. I hugged the handlebars, staying low as I righted the bike as it wobbled. I turned, only to see a nondescript SUV coming at us fast again, ready to shunt us off the road or run right over us.

Great, just when I thought the day couldn't get any worse.

"Wyrmlings," I screamed. Dancer turned then sped up.

He had a lot to answer for. I knew they weren't just angry about Dragon. They had a score to settle with Dancer for whatever went down years ago in his homeland and now they'd found him nothing would stop them getting their revenge.

Well, if they wanted him they'd have to go through me first. We were friends and friends stick together.

It was just a shame they hadn't left it a while, I was kind of pre-occupied.

We weaved through rush-hour traffic, always moving well in the well-laid out roads that circled Cardiff, then were past a slip road and the way ahead was clear. We sped up and tried to lose the wyrmlings that would kill us before the virus did if we weren't careful and very lucky.

It was hard to feel like luck was on my side right now, but at least I had my own teeth and hair, so that was something.

Running on Empty

An hour later and we were both running on fumes. The bikes and us, too. We pulled in to a petrol station and filled up the gleaming tanks on the monster bikes, drawing admiring glances from men standing at their cars, envy written large on their faces. I could imagine what they were thinking. That they'd love the freedom, the chance to ride on a mean machine without a care in the world, probably wondering if we were in a bizarre cult biker gang as we certainly looked nothing like your average biker.

But they'd forget us as soon as they had such thoughts, which was just as well as we were both utter wrecks. Suits torn, slashed, ripped, and covered in the fetid goop of all manner of magical abusers, numerous wounds festering. Dancer had awful dark bags under his eyes and a wild look like a rabbit caught in the headlights. He constantly tugged at his livid forearm, now swollen badly. Red and blue and purple and green.

I would have looked a lot worse. Hell, in one day I'd fallen from my kitchen into a weird dragon netherworld, rode said dragon, had one helluva fight at Council HQ, got bitten, escaped. Oh, and been to Delilah's, run around naked, worn dodgy sportswear, eaten amazing curry, and on and on it went.

Was that right? Had it been one day? It felt like too much to fit into so few hours but I was sure it had all happened today. My thoughts were clouded, though, my mind a mess of confusion as I tried to put the day into order.

It didn't matter. All that mattered was that we stayed alive and dealt with the current set of problems facing us. I hated to admit it, but this was just about the worst thing that had happened to me, ever. I couldn't see a way out of it, not in time, anyway, as the only way I knew to stop the virus taking control involved magic on a whole other level to what I possessed and right this moment I possessed about zero.

Slowly, I was recharging, but it would take time and it would take rest. Lots of rest. And sleep. And food. And more rest. And a cuddle. A shower would have been nice, too. And another cuddle. Damn, who was I kidding? Mostly, I wanted to curl up in a ball and cry, or rage at the world and scream, "It's not fair!" But I got it together—just—and held the rage inside.

We walked in a daze into the small store to pay, only to find it was like a mini supermarket, more and more of them having popped up over recent years. More generic stuff, no independents left now, just places full of brand coffee and brand sandwiches as boring and bland as you can get. Still, people seemed to like it, and I guess we all want the familiar. The same coffee, same snacks, to know exactly what we'll get. Right about now, all that sounded like bliss.

Still not speaking, walking like the undead we were soon to be, we paid for fuel and bought the brand coffee and sandwiches and I didn't even argue about the astronomical price I was so tired and in need of sustenance.

We took our purchases outside and shambled over to a picnic bench at the side of the building. Silent, we munched on meatball sandwiches and drank scalding coffee. I ignored the warning on the side—it was supposed to be hot. It was coffee!

"So, zombies, eh?" I said, glancing at my leg and trying not to scream at the injustice of it all.

"Yeah. Zombies. At least most of our people got out. Guess they had sense enough to run away before the wyrmlings arrived in force."

"That's something, right?"

"Hmm." Dancer tugged at his tie, loosening it. "And Dragon, he's gone, so that's good. Ah, hell, Spark, I'm sorry I dragged you into all this."

"Hey, you weren't to know. And besides, it was my choice. You know what?"

"What?"

"I'm glad I came back. This is who I am, I've accepted that now. Magic's a part of me, and apart from the getting bitten thing it all worked out fine."

"Yeah, apart from the getting bitten thing."

"Hmm."

We finished up in silence. I guess it's just not the kind of thing there's much to talk about when you're so exhausted you can't even begin to think about it properly. Just being still and quiet for a while gave us back a little of ourselves. Allowed us to regroup and muster what strength remained. But we had to have a plan, and we couldn't stay long. The wyrmlings, the Romanian wyrmlings that were out not just for revenge for Dragon but for whatever Dancer had been involved in all those years ago, would catch up with us soon, and then we'd be toast.

"Okay, what's the plan? You said you had an idea, so now would be a good time to give me some good news about all this." I prayed Dancer had a way to stop this, and something inside told me he genuinely did. I hoped it involved no amputating of limbs. I'd grown attached to my legs over the years. It let me have two feet to wear my winklepickers. Plus the whole walking thing, I'd grown accustomed to that, too.

Dancer moved his empty cup aside and rested his arms on the table. He was shaking, and his arm looked worse. I knew I was the same. My leg burned hot and itched something terrible.

"I know someone. Someone who can help. If we get to her, she'll be able to deal with this."

"Who is it? And how will she deal with it?"

"That doesn't matter. Just trust me, okay?"

"Dancer, Boss, I trust you, but come on, you have to give me more than this."

"Spark, this is for your own good. I can't talk about her, or tell you exactly where she is, as, well, she's rather secretive and if I say her name she'll know. If I say much of anything about her at all she'll know, and then she won't help. Understand?"

"She's a private person? I get it. But why the secrecy? She a wacko?"

Dancer glanced around nervously as if she was about to step out from behind the building and go nuts on us. Who was this woman? "No, she's not a wacko. Okay, maybe a little, but she can help. You have to trust me on this. But you know as well as I do that we don't have long to get this dealt with. I can feel it already and I'm fighting it, but in another day or so it'll be too late and once it takes hold properly there's no going back."

"I know. I'm doing all I can but it would help if I wasn't so drained."

"I hear you. But we have to, Spark. We have to stop it getting too deep inside us or we'll be the bloody walking dead." Dancer got wearily to his feet. "I can't believe it," he raged. "I finally get into a good position in life and this happens. I never catch a break."

"Feel better now?"

"Yeah, a little."

"Good, because shit's about to get nasty." I pointed at the SUV heading toward the service station and tried not to wince as I joined Dancer, taking deep breaths and readying myself for action. "Time to go, and fast."

"Okay. We're heading north, that's all I can say for now. Follow me, and don't get lost."

"I won't. This is a big ask, you know? I'm trusting you here, Dancer. This is my life at stake. I have a family now, Kate and Mithnite, not to mention Grandma. I don't want to miss out on what was looking to be a happy future now I'm back with mistress magic, too."

"We'll be fine. Let's go."

As the SUV approached, stuck behind a line of cars edging forward to refuel, we got on the bikes and took to the roads.

We roared away. I knew they'd be after us.

A Rush

Something happened as we hammered the bikes and sailed along the motorway, heading north to who knew where to meet our mystery woman. Not only did the caffeine and the food kick in—offering clarity and a much needed energy boost—but I felt my magic levels top up like the bike's tank.

I was filling back up minute by minute. My call to the Empty, my craving for magic to course through my veins and swell the ink finally answered. It's amazing how habits become ingrained, and for a hundred years I'd become accustomed to being on death's door after intense magic use, needing weeks, sometimes months to recover from enforcer jobs, close to death and good for nothing. So, that's what I expected this time, but it wasn't the case at all.

Even after all I'd been through, I was recovering quickly. Drained, but not empty inside like a husk of a dark magic enforcer. I was different now and it took some getting used to. There was a background thrum of magic that could not be depleted. Not a reserve so much as an innate ability, a hallmark of true Hidden creatures.

Regardless of the fact I'd ignored magic over the last five years, this thing inside of me had grown. It had strengthened, it had solidified, it had become a true part of me after I'd awoken it in my time of need in Tokyo.

Faz Pound was true Hidden.

What had Dragon said of this gift from the giant? That I was immortal as long as I didn't get myself killed. Yes, I could be killed, but I was also no longer a human being who could wield elemental forces. I was something else. A magical being who had an undying spark—haha—of eternal life and power at the core of my being.

It was stirring. Drawing energy in from the Empty without me even having to think about it. This was how I always sensed true Hidden to be. No matter how much I drained them, stole their magic away, there was an untouchable core. Like a dense backup battery that was impenetrable and immutable. I thought back to my time in the skinner's room and the lump I'd discovered nestling beside my heart. Wound up tight and waiting to be unleashed.

This was me now, and as I spat out flies and tried to see while the wind sucked at my eyelids, my spirits soared as magic engulfed me, supercharging my battered body, shunting fantastical chemical combinations around my body as fast as my heart could pump them. Battling and raging against the virus that was the enemy. The deep ache and burn in my thigh eased off until I could almost imagine I'd beaten it for good, banished the infection to a sealed-off place inside where it could do no harm. There was sadness, too, as I knew all I'd done was slow the inevitable.

Still, better than nothing, right? When you've been bitten by the undead you take what you can and don't complain. Or not much, anyway.

We roared past junctions, overtook when we could, but slowed down when we hit traffic as we closed on Birmingham. We were safe for now. No way would an SUV be able to get through the traffic and reach us, and besides, the last thing we wanted was to be stopped by the police.

It was a relief. My face felt battered. I'd consumed more bugs than was healthy even for a bird, and my eyes were half-glued together in a weird way from squinting for so long. We needed gear if we were to stay on the bikes. A helmet, or sunglasses at the very least. True, there was an amazing sense of freedom, but it was marred by the almost overpowering feeling of vulnerability as you hurtled past massive lumps of metal at seventy miles-per-hour with nothing but a retro suit between you and the asphalt.

The bike throbbed between my painful thighs and I wondered why I'd gone so long without owning a bike. Ethelbald had done a serious job on them, too. The chrome gleamed, the seat leather was dark and thick, and there were more bespoke parts than off-the-shelf. He was gonna be pissed, I knew that much. Why?

Because there wasn't a hope in hell that the bikes wouldn't be trashed at some point—I was surprised we'd managed to ride for so long already. He thinks of them as his babies, and woe-betide any customer that treats his creations with anything but love and attention.

We slowed in a traffic bottleneck and pulled up alongside each other. Dancer wasn't looking good, even by his standards, and I refused to look in my mirrors, however shiny and chrome-lined they were, for fear of what I'd see.

"We need to get off the main roads," I shouted. "It's just a matter of time before we get stopped for not wearing helmets."

"Spark, we're the invisible men, nobody will call it in. Look." Dancer nodded at a guy in a Subaru one lane across from us. He glanced at us, frowned at our appearance, then promptly looked away. We were already forgotten.

"I know we're nigh on invisible, but it only takes someone to act quickly before thinking too much, or for a cop car to go past, and it could get nasty." It wasn't likely, we truly are ghosts to Regulars, but why take the chance? "And besides, we need to make sure the wyrmlings don't find us. We need rest, and food. More food. And sleep. You do know the kind of day I've had, right?"

"Hey, mine hasn't exactly been a picnic," he protested.

At the mention of food my stomach somersaulted. "Let's just get off at the next junction and take it easy."

"Fine," he agreed.

We crawled through the traffic. How could people do this every damn day? The same in the morning and the evening? It would drive me nuts. Guess that's the sacrifices we make to feed ourselves, put a roof over our heads and our families'. Respect where it's due; I couldn't imagine anything worse.

Fifteen minutes later, we were sailing down quiet lanes, as rural as it gets. Hard to imagine that a short distance away the billboards screamed at distracted drivers and the skyline was nothing but skyscrapers and a maze of roads that led nowhere I wanted to go.

The sight of fields and hedgerows calmed my mind and body, and for the first time since we got rather violently booted from Council HQ I felt a glimmer of hope.

Then everything went dark and I felt the zombie virus steal my sight.

Oops

"Haha." I laughed at my own idiocy. It wasn't the zombie virus taking me over, we'd just entered a tunnel of dense oak trees overhanging the road and were plunged into darkness. I flipped on the full beam and chased Dancer's tail lights, emerging into dying rays of golden sunlight as day got ready to give up its warmth to the cold of the English night. We had hours yet, but dusk was fast-approaching and we would have to slow if we were to remain safe.

A noxious smell of rotten eggs assaulted my freezing nostrils and I glanced down at the handlebars.

"Wotcha, Spark, got any... Ack, ugh. Gross," moaned Intus as she stuck out a tongue that kept on unfolding and scraped dead insects from the bright red thing with tiny but deadly claws.

"Hey, Intus. Um, I'm kind of riding a motorbike at the moment. Can this wait?"

"Wait? No, it can't wait," she replied testily, ears flapping wildly and tail the same as the wind battered her three inch body. She gripped tight, her incredible strength making the bike veer.

"Whoa! Careful. If we crash I'll be dead."

"You big baby. A bit of dying never hurt anyone."

"Actually, it totally has, loads of times," I said, knowing it was an argument I could never win no matter how often I tried to explain the difference between a human's life and an immortal, demonic imp's.

"Whatever. Look, can we talk?"

"Talk? About what?"

"Got an, er, serious problem. Someone's been nicking the kids. I'm down about twenty of the little buggers. Um, I mean, darling implings. Illus won't let me hear the end of it. Says I gotta find 'em, and quick. That it makes us look bad. I'm sure they'll turn up, but you know how Illus likes to make sure we always have the right number. Stupid, but there you go." She shrugged her tiny shoulders and smiled her wide and cheeky grin, although how she pulls it off and looks cute whilst also looking so terrifying, if in miniature, is beyond me. Maybe I'm biased, or maybe it's a size thing. Not that I'd ever mention that to her, of course.

"Damn, I'm so sorry, Intus. Anything I can do to help, just say the word."

"Cool, I was hoping you'd say that." She smiled at me and my heart sank.

"Oh, no, I didn't mean that."

It was too late. Me and my big mouth.

Intus clicked her fingers even as I spoke. The world split into a million parts, the veil between our world and the infernal underworld—hell, Impland, or whatever or wherever imps live for eternity—soaked through into my reality. Up ahead were green hills and a darkening sky, but a layer of red death descended from above like a dodgy fade-in. As though red paint dripped down the canvas of my world, raucous and manic laughter echoing through from a realm I was never meant to know or see, let alone be a part of. It came down faster and faster, wiping away the world.

Then time froze.

My bike stopped, and I turned to Dancer only to discover he was frozen. A snapshot of an exhausted man who looked like a funeral director, his oiled hair wild from the buffeting of the wind. Bits of insect stuck to his face, eyes almost closed as he squinted. Suit trashed, bite on his forearm exposed and looking all kinds of nasty, like a snake bite times a thousand. The exhaust fumes trailed behind him in a weird static montage, tiny droplets of fuel sparkling.

Then everything I knew and understood vanished and I was no longer in my world.

I was in Intus'.

Eek!

She was on my shoulder, and I was standing in a ravine maybe five feet deep so I had a view of Impland as seen almost from their height, give or take a foot.

My eyes took in the scene. My mind reacted by shutting down. I screamed, and millions of tiny imp heads turned at the sound as it echoed through valleys of mismatched socks, bounced off the mountains of lost keys, and made thousands of pairs of underwear vibrate on the imps' work benches where they were busy picking apart the stitching so they'd rip at the most inopportune moment when returned to unsuspecting owners.

Then I lost my sanity and the gibbering of countless alien tongues, in a demonic language I could never hope to understand, all chattered manically in my mind simultaneously.

The last thing I remember before I lost even the vestige of sanity was Intus up close, peeling back an eyelid and prodding my eyeball as she said, "Oops."

Damn right, oops.

Lost Implings

I spat out the noxious liquid, so bitter and foul it made anything the Chemist had ever given me taste like a fancy cocktail.

"Just drink it," ordered Intus, tipping the test tube of liquid—red, of course—up high so the poison hit my throat again.

"Gah," I choked. "Is this lava?"

Intus tilted her oversized—it's all relative—head to one side and peered at me suspiciously. The fact she was at eye level meant I must have been lying on the ground, my head sideways, or ripped off, or something equally demonic and stupid. "Of course it's not lava. You don't drink lava, you bathe in it."

"Ack. Uck. Aggle. Ah, stupid me."

"Right?" she said knowingly, then upended the rest of the vial.

With no choice, the liquid dried out my mouth like it had been set fire to, burned its way down my scalded throat, hit my stomach and erupted into what I can only describe as feeling like hell itself had been miniaturized and thrust through my skin into my belly. Then the party really got started.

Speaking of hells in miniature...

My vision cleared and my mind stopped screaming about the terrors of all things imp related. The chittering and chattering of nasty beasties that made Poe's imaginings pale in comparison fluttered away back to the dark recesses of my mind, and the door slammed shut on them, leaving me clear-headed and light of limb. I felt fab.

For less time than it took to scream. Then Round Two kicked in.

Intus, and about a thousand other imps who appeared in a cloud of vomit-inducing stink, took a few steps back as I thrashed about wildly. I expected to pulverize them to smithereens as I flapped and kicked and generally acted like I'd been poisoned by a so-called friend in the netherworlds, but I didn't. I watched in horror, mind numb against such an impossible reality, as my arm shrank and kept on shrinking.

The rest of me followed suit. Head, legs, torso, the lot. All of it shrank and it felt like my insides weren't catching up fast enough to deal with the new, diminutive Faz Pound.

I may have screamed. I may have ranted. I may have shouted abuse. Then it was over. I was still me, but tiny. An itsy-bitsy Faz Pound. Intus walked up to me as the other imps wandered off, bored. Heading back to work, or what they called work, when it looked more like fun throwing socks about and sliding down mountains of keys that soared up high until lost to cloud—again, red.

"Intus, put me back to my right size this instant. And get me out of here. I've got things to do. Important things." Then it hit me. My bike, the speed, the lack of me on it. Was the bike already in a ditch? Had it crashed into Dancer? How would Intus return me without killing me? More to the point, how had she got me here in the first place?

Was I really here? Or had she just done something gnarly and impish to my mind?

"You said you'd help. Anything. Remember?" Intus came close and stood beside me, shoulder to shoulder. We were the same size, give or take the extra hair on my head.

"Yeah, but I didn't mean this. How is this even possible? Isn't this off-limits? And what about my size? Ugh, there's something I need to tell you." I glanced down at my torn suit—still the same, but the perfect size for a small action figure. I prodded my leg, pulled at the material, but it was just bare flesh. Clean, unmarked, definitely no bite mark. I was whole again. Searching inside, I felt good. On top of the world although I was far beneath it. No infection, just magic. Lots of magic.

"The weird zombie thing, right? Don't worry about it," she said, eyes reflecting madness, twinkling with delight. "We don't have zombies here, can't. Imps only."

"But I'm not an imp," I moaned, utterly at a loss.

"I know that," she said, way too close for comfort.

It's one thing having an imp as a friend when they can sit in you palm, another thing entirely when they're full-size—or you're small, same thing—and you can see every detail of them up close and way too personal. Her smile was like a shark's. Rows of teeth gleaming huge and monstrous. Her claws made her stretched arms appear almost regular length, and don't even get me started on the madness that seemed to scream for release from beneath taut skin, or the tail, or the strange bulge and... Ugh, enough.

"So, what gives?"

"I made a few changes. We have our ways. And don't sweat about getting home, it's all taken care of."

I was going to ask what that meant, but thought better of it. Best I didn't know, not yet. "Intus, this is nuts. Humans can't be here, it's not possible."

"Aha," Intus jumped around excitedly, "but you aren't human now, and you offered," she reminded me. Again.

"The giant thing?" I said with a sigh.

"Yup." She smiled a smug smile. She's good at it, got her smugness down to an art.

"Fine," I said, knowing this was a battle I wouldn't win. "Let's find the kids. Um, is it always this hot?"

"Sorry, Spark, I must have given you the wrong potion. I didn't realize it would make you utterly idiotic."

"Look, I was just asking."

"Hey, you wanna see my house?"

"Er, sure. Why not?"

There was a very good reason why not, as I soon found out.

Ugh

"Jesus, fucking, holy, mothering shit, fuck, ugh," I continued—the bad language had been going for some time. Sorry about that, just keeping it real. Anyway, you weren't there.

"You like it, then?"

My head spun wildly and I sank into what passed for a chair in these here parts, ignoring the scalding of the semi-molten, semi-sentient furniture, surprised to find my suit wasn't burning.

"Ugh," I managed again, which was better than continuing with the swearing. I'd exhausted all the words I knew, anyway, and had progressed to making new ones up. I got some good ones, too.

"Wanna see the pool?" Intus wandered over to one of the endless screens that ran on and on in every direction, receding into the distance until too small to see. There must have been millions of them, maybe infinite.

"Maybe later. I'm guessing it's lava based?"

"How did you know? You been peeking? Been here before?"

"Just a wild guess," I moaned. I was doing a lot of that lately. Muttering, too. I was mastering the mutter real quick.

The house was less a conventional space than an infinite sea of chaos, somehow still managing to be rammed with more unusual, mostly unfathomable items than I'd ever imagined, and I'd imagined a lot of weird stuff when it came to Intus.

There were rocks of all sizes, strange elongated things like clubs made from jagged shards of cooled lava three times our size, and so many weapons of bizarre shape I didn't know what to look at next or whether to look at anything at all. Apparently, lots of it was either for the kids to play with or for gardening. Only a few choice weapons were for Intus' work as she, too, was an enforcer. Just like one in every five other imps. They get into a lot of mischief and lose control, so the more sensible ones—yes, Intus was one of them—had to be constantly on guard to clean up when things went haywire.

Good job their wayward nature is mostly benign. Comprising getting carried away with hiding things, re-arranging cupboards, moving chairs a little bit, or messing with the height so you sit down only to find it's slightly shorter than usual, but you don't quite realize, and wonder why you cracked your arse as you sat down the same as you have thousands of times before.

Unaware that imps have been working hard to saw off maybe a quarter inch from the legs.

There were weird slabs protruding from walls that acted as dividers, hiding more madness—apparently cots for the kids or somewhere to get stretched out if they were feeling short, or their arms weren't growing fast enough—and on and on the nuttiness went.

I couldn't take it. The whole realm was so different it was impossible to focus on, let alone make any proper sense of.

And that was without the damn screens. I glanced from one to another, and another, mind in a state of shock and utter confusion.

"Um, that's me, right? From the beginning?" I got excited and searched the screens, hoping for a glimpse of when I was young. When I was with my parents. Then I caught sight of Kate and Mithnite at our home, sitting at the kitchen table, talking and looking worried. Kate continually picking up her phone and checking it.

Hell, she'd be worried sick.

Click.

I turned to see Intus with an infinite remote control, a big red power button with her claw firmly on it. All the screens were blank.

"Sorry, Spark, but you know the rules. You can't see that."

"No, I don't. I thought I did but now I don't. Have you got my whole life there? Can you see it all?"

Intus scratched her head and said, "Yes. But no. Um, sort of. It's because we're linked. You know I always know what's happening in your life, but sometimes I arrive early, or late, not quite when you need me. Well, this is why. It's jumbled sometimes, depending on your emotions, my mood, the luck of the draw. Lots of things," she waved away the notion. "But, usually, it's what's going on right about now. But in your time," she added hurriedly, "we don't do time here. Not much point when you have eternity. Which, trust me, seems like a very long time if you keep checking the clock."

"So you won't show me?"

Intus shook her head. "Can't. It's against the rules."

I sighed. I was getting really good at that, too. "Okay, fine. Let's find these kids. Where's the rest of them? The ones that aren't lost?"

That was my second really stupid question of the day. Or was it the third? I lose track.

Attack of the Nasties

"What's that for?" asked an impling. At least I assumed it was judging by the diaper and the way it kept sucking on its claw between tugging at my finger.

"It's my finger. It's for... er, pointing and stuff."

"What's that for?" asked another darling impling with a lollipop stuck to its cheek, pulling hard at my hair. "It's for, er, keeping my head warm."

"But what is it? Can I have it?"

"No, me, me, I want it."

"No, it's mine."

"Mummy, the ugly pink thing won't let me have the hair. I want some."

And on and on it went. Hundreds of them, all pulling and tugging and asking questions and yanking and poking and licking. Ugh, the licking.

"Quiet!" roared Intus in the deep baritone I was getting used to as it seemed even I spoke like that down here.

Silence descended for about a heartbeat and then they all burst out crying, molten tears of fire that scorched the rock carpet and pitted the surface like acid —it probably was, I'm not really up on baby imps and their fluids.

It was deafening. The bawling gnawed at my mind and ate away my marrow, leaving every nerve exposed. I wanted to crawl into a hole and let someone chop off all my bits and post them to the acid factory.

Intus turned to me and said, "You could have let them have your hair. You don't need it."

"Of course I do. It's for..." Okay, she had a point. I didn't *need* it, but I liked the way it looked and it really did keep my head warm. Yes, I could have worn a hat or let it grow back, but c'mon.

"See what I have to put up with? This is why I like to come visit. Uh-oh, I think I'm having another one."

"Another one, what?" I asked with dread, knowing full well what she meant but hoping beyond hope I was wrong.

"A baby. Another impling. You wanna help? Wanna see the miracle happen?"

I backed off, arms up, already going *lalalala* in my mind. "No way. Absolutely not. You, er, go about your birth business, I'll look after the kids. Damn." What was wrong with me? How could I say such a thing? See how flustered I was?

What happened next was a lesson in what the words "truly infinite" mean. It was as if time stretched out in one long line of never-ending, nightmarish questions. There were constant pleas for potty, and nappy changes, tantrums because they wanted yum-yums and more potty, and more tickles, and lollies.

Some wanted a lava bath, others wanted to play on the key slide. Others wanted to play bury the pink blob in the Pit of Infinite Pain—I skipped it—and there were tears and there were screams and then, when I'd just about lost my mind and thought I must have done something utterly despicable in my life, and was dead now and in the worst kind of hell, worse than anyone had ever imagined in the whole history of humankind, it was quiet.

They sat, utterly still. A massive circle of them hemming me in from all directions, no means of escape. Hundreds of imp children of various sizes in numerous states of undress. Some with the full leathers, heavy on the buckles, always dungarees, some just in nappies or wearing a pair of pants on their head—leather, of course—or pouring things over their heads. Sticking fingers up noses—usually their siblings'—but at least they were quiet.

"Hey, Spark, wanna meet the new arrival?" asked Intus as she came from who knew where.

"Ssh," I said, and every child turned back from her interruption to me, where I sat, cross-legged, the kids' eyes wide and lost in wonder at the tale Uncle Spark was weaving.

Intus plonked herself down with the newborn in her arms and as something I didn't want to think about expanded on her usually flat chest—all imps look the same, no sign of sexual body parts ever normally in evidence—I continued.

*

"...and then the dragon smashed through the ceiling with us still on its back and we found ourselves out of the wondrous, crumbling lair and back up in our own world." I looked up only to find that all the implings were curled up in balls on the red, dusty ground, snoring loudly, twitching as they dreamed of dragons and looking utterly serene.

"What happened next?" asked Intus, rocking the baby in her arms.

"You know what happened," I whispered.

"Yeah, but it's not the same as having a story."

Several children stirred and began to ask questions.

"Uncle Spark, did you get any paninis?"

"What's boobies?"

"Can we get a dragon?"

"Ssh," I said, finger to my lips. "I'll finish the story next time. Okay?" The implings nodded and lay their heads back down, fast asleep once more.

I nodded to Intus and we crept away, leaving them to their slumber.

"Wow, Spark, you've got a real talent for this," said Intus, admiringly.

"You think? Haha, it was kinda cool."

"Absolutely. They've never all gone to sleep at the same time. Never." Intus turned to look back at the sleeping forms of her children, shaking her head in wonder.

"You've definitely got your hands full. Come on, let's go find the missing ones and then I need to get back to my own world. You can't do this again, you know that, right?"

"Sorry, I know. It's just..."

"Yeah, I offered."

"No, not just that. But they're my kids, Spark. I know I moan about them and act like I'm not bothered, but trust me, when you have your own, you'll understand. They drive you out of your mind but you love 'em, understand?"

"Of course. Come on, where were they last?"

Intus led me off into the madness and the children continued to snore.

The Lost Ones

Life is so strange at times. That one act gave me a peculiar feeling inside. Yes, they were little terrors and I'd nearly been driven crazy by them, but it was immensely satisfying telling a story and watching their little demonic faces, rapt, their imaginations running wild until finally they succumbed to sleep.

I felt paternal, understood this was the one thing missing from my life. Don't get me wrong, I was happy with Kate, no question about it, but children, yeah, it had its appeal.

Was that selfish? To even consider having children when we lived the kind of lives we did? An enforcer and a vampire, the perfect parents. I felt foolish for even thinking about being a dad. Me off on my next job, getting into endless trouble. Risking life, limb, and sanity. And Kate, hunting her next meal. Killing some corrupt soul so she could feed the addiction and live another day? We couldn't be parents, we were wild and strange things and didn't deserve such a gift.

Or did we? I'd thought about this so much since Japan, and my conversation with Kate concerning it had led to nothing but heartache for her and confusion for us both. Neither of us even knowing if we actually wanted children. But this storytelling, it changed something. Made me understand that there was something missing inside and it was the continuation of my family line. Heck, I was the last, and if I had no children the bloodline would die whenever I did. It's a sobering thought, but also one tinged with selfishness. I wanted a family of my own. I wanted to be there for the little guy or gal, and ensure they had a life I could never have—one with parents. And that was the real rub—Mommy and Daddy could be wiped out at any moment.

It's the primitive urge to procreate, nothing more, I told myself, but that didn't change the fact I felt a sense of wholeness telling a tale to a bunch of demonic tearaways. What would it be like if I did the same with a child of my own?

Silly, as it was very unlikely Kate could ever bear children, and even if we found a way, she wasn't sure if she ever wanted them and neither was I when I got right down to it.

The thought both appealed and repulsed me. The loss of freedom, the loss of the wildness, the loss of my edge. Would I be ineffective if I had the weight of responsibility hanging over me at all times? Probably. Look what had happened recently. Getting sucked through our own kitchen floor, dragons and zombies and all kinds of madness. If a child had been present then it would have died, and how would I feel about myself if I ever let that happen?

Above all else, that didn't bear thinking about. No, I was being utterly selfish even considering such a thing, so I did my best to put it out of my mind and focused on the job at hand. Which was finding Intus' kids quick-smart and getting the hell out of this insanity before I lost the plot completely.

I knew it would be like this, knew it would be some stupid thing she'd overlooked, so as we peered into the smoky interior of the cave, where the children had apparently been playing with the scorching steam that hissed up from the bowels of their home, I asked, "What were they doing here?"

"Dunno," shrugged Intus. "Some game or other. You know how kids are."

"Not really, no."

"Oh, er. I've looked for them everywhere, shouted and called and threatened and screamed, but they're gone, Spark. They could be anywhere."

"It's a big place, right?"

"Duh, it's infinite."

"This may be a stupid question, but what's their absolute favorite thing to eat?"

"To eat? Well, they like Marmite, and salt, and they love slate. It's the layers, they can't get enough of it."

"Okay, here's the plan," I whispered into Intus' ear, and once we'd agreed we were set.

We sat down and I said, "Oh, Intus, that sounds like a wonderful idea. I love me some Welsh slate. It's just a shame your children aren't here to share it, as it's totally amazing. Look at the bits, I think maybe that's moss, too. You know what? I'm gonna smother mine with Marmite. Yum-yum."

"Now, Spark, don't go stuffing yourself too full, you know how heavy it sits in your belly."

"Okay, fair enough. Now, what shall we do with the leftovers? Shall I just chuck it?"

"Yup, may as well," said Intus, sounding about as believable as if she'd refused the offer of new socks still with the cardboard bands around them.

"Okay, then. I'm going to throw it away right now."

"No," came a chorus of voices from the cave as the kids came rushing forward through the scalding, sulfur-heavy steam, the vents belching out great geysers of the stuff.

They clamored around us, pestering for slate, asking where it was and had the pink man thing really thrown it away.

Intus began to scold the children but I knew her heart wasn't in it, that she was glad they were home. After they'd been sent on their way, told to go back to their siblings and not to hide like that again, I understood what this had all been about.

"You're a sneaky so-and-so, you know that, right?"

Intus' ears pointed up, erect and proud as she smiled. "I know."

"All of this, just to show me what it's like? They weren't lost at all, were they? You knew where they were, just used it as an excuse to get me down here to meet them and get all fatherly."

"Who, me? As if I'd do such a thing," said Intus, protesting, trying, and failing, to hold back a chuckle. One thing she is not is a good actor.

"Haha, well, thanks, Intus. I think. You know you must never do this again?"

"Desperate times call for desperate measures, Spark."

"Time to go?"

"Yup. I'm in enough trouble as it is."

"I bet," I said, and then Intus handed me a tiny vial. "It's symbolic, right?"

"Of course. You don't think drinking a potion can really shrink you or allow you to come and go from here, do you?"

"No, of course not. But I get it, it's what it does to the mind."

"Wrong. It's out of your control, Spark. It's all down to me. I click my fingers and—"

My body was consumed with searing heat that felt like my flesh was stripped from my bones and all was darkness for a moment.

I opened my eyes, only to see a tree right in front of me. I righted the bike and glanced to the left where Dancer was staring at me, astonished, wondering why I'd veered when we were on a straight stretch of the lane.

Everything was familiar. I think I'd been gone for maybe half a second if that.

Intus is a true friend, if rather unconventional in her ways at times. But that's what mates are for, to show you things and help you when you're in a quandary about the course of your life.

It would have been nice if she'd also stopped the zombie virus, but they can't really interfere in the events of this world, and besides, what would she watch on TV if I didn't get up to such nonsense on a regular basis?

I got the bike under control, sighed with relief, then turned to check on Dancer who'd fallen back a little to give me room, oblivious to what had just gone down.

"Bugger," I shouted, and he turned to see what I saw. "Here come the wyrmlings."

We gave the bikes some serious throttle and hurtled through country lanes somewhere in the Midlands as the sun set.

The Need for Speed

I hunched down low, willing the bike to move faster even though I was already going a hundred miles an hour. I wiggled my body, just to check Intus had done nothing weird, as I gave full throttle and the engine growled at the punishment. We were on a long straight stretch now, but I knew I was going too fast, was asking for trouble. But what could I do? Get splatted by the wyrmlings or risk coming off? I risked the speed.

Dancer caught me up and we acknowledged each other nervously. This was not good. A quick glance behind told me they were still closing—we were gonna be toast.

Knowing there was nothing to lose, I called to the Empty, hoping beyond hope it would answer my call this time. Damn, but something hurt. A good sign? Maybe. As I reached deeper, I finally found the connection and magic poured into my system with a sharp jolt like a dam had burst. The energy was unstoppable. It gushed inside, engorging my ink as it spiraled and spun around my body, recharging energy centers and communing with my innate magic, completing me, making me whole again.

Ah, my friend. My enemy, my curse, and my only way to feel truly alive. I welcomed the despicable magic like it had been years since we were last joined, rather than hours, and then it began.

My eyes snapped to black like the flick of a bat's wing, dark and nasty as the oil in the engine, and with a crack of magic louder than the bike misfiring, I blasted a white flash of jagged magic at the car and it hit, dead on.

I smiled in satisfaction as the front wheels lifted off the road then came back down with a thud and a grinding of metal. The extreme force made the rear lift high in the air and then the whole vehicle was airborne.

It tumbled end over end. The SUV crashed down, but the force of the magic gave it immense kinetic energy and it flipped up high, gaining speed and spinning faster and faster, jagged lines of wayward magic sparking in all directions. Out of control and imbued with desperation and too much force as I'd not metered the magic properly. My smile turned to panic as I realized the car's momentum meant it was gaining on us—we'd be flattened any second.

Here it comes, here it comes.

I tried to crawl inside my skin as I watched the vehicle arc even higher, and then it was past us, crashing to the road in front of us and skidding sideways down the road. No time to brake or swerve to avoid it, I shot magic at the asphalt, willing it to rise and provide a ramp.

We hit, simultaneously, the rough rubble hardly making for a smooth launch. I soared up high and over the wreck, handlebars wobbling, bike almost out of control as I clung to it for dear life, realizing I hadn't thought about landing and that if I didn't straighten the bike up I'd be crushed to death.

I forced my body to relax as the wind howled into my face, and stabilized the bike a moment before I landed with a jolt, right on the broken center line. Dancer landed a moment later, wobbled terribly, and I thought he would crash for sure, but he leaned forward, went with it, and eventually got it under control.

The car burst into flames behind us as we hammered the throttle and roared away from the heat and death.

Dusk hit like a hammer had smacked the sun down beneath the horizon and I switched on the bike's headlights. Cat's eyes glinted like silent sentinels, keeping track of a dark magic enforcer who wanted to just ride and ride and for nothing bad to happen and for the road to never end.

But there is no peace, there is no freedom, not even an illusion of such an elusive pursuit, and just like my life, the road was running out. An unexpected sharp bend meant I eased off the power and took the turn with a skid as I hit the brakes. My knee grazed the ground, and only the fat tires saved me from skidding off entirely. Dancer was right behind me, peeling his bike back to vertical with easy control.

Back on the straight, we were up over sixty in three seconds flat. I wondered if I'd find peace, the chance to rest and go home, ever again.

As if on cue, the bike spluttered and slowed. I stared in horror as the fuel gauge vibrated then stuck on empty—damn, talk about bad timing.

With a final groan, all power died and I was coasting.

I jumped off the bike and tried not to cry as it crashed into a low stone wall and finally fell over, paintwork ruined on my newfound pride and joy.

Dancer stopped up ahead, then turned and headed back to me. "What happened?"

"It ran out of fuel," I said, nonplussed.

"Thought you'd filled it up?"

"I did," I said, scratching my head. I walked over to the bike, righted it and kicked out the stand. There was a hole in the tank. It must have been from the explosion, meaning I was lucky to still be alive.

"What now?" asked Dancer.

Before I could answer, we heard a roar behind us. No prizes for guessing what it was, or who was inside.

"Guess I ride pillion." I hopped on and with no time to mourn the loss of such a fine machine, I turned and readied myself as a car screeched around the corner. It slowed when the occupants saw us in the middle of the road, then the driver put his foot down and came at us, fast and loud. Damn, but this was one powerful car.

Dancer said, "Hold on," and he gave the bike all he could.

For a moment, just a moment, mind you, I missed Intus' home world. I could have finished my story.

A New Plan

Riding pillion is scary, especially when you're sat behind your boss and he seems intent on killing you by driving you off the edge of the nearest cliff.

Dancer pushed the bike to its limits, and having no control pushed my nerves likewise. I focused on reducing the magic, allowed my eyes to fade to regular blue and hunkered down, the only benefit to my position being I wasn't pummeled by the air and Dancer was getting all the bugs.

Magic receded and I was myself once more.

But there was no sickness, no cramping and moaning as the Empty came calling. No, I just ached. A deep, dull throb inside I was unsure was an aftereffect of magic, general hurt, or more than likely the result of the infection taking hold with renewed vigor now magic no longer held it at bay.

We drove on, mindful of the darkening sky. No streetlights here, just long stretches of road connecting villages, unsuited for the raw speed we maintained.

Inevitably, we had to slow. The road became potholed and dangerous. Our speed was just asking for us to crash at some point. We had to act sensibly, so Dancer eased off to a respectable speed and we both breathed a sigh of relief.

Adrenaline levels adjusted and it was only then I realized quite how manic I'd been feeling. Had that just happened? Cars flipping and exploding as we tore away? Wowzers! That was some serious action hero stuff. And Intus, surely that was a dream? It was impossible to tell. Had I lost the plot for a while, events overloading my senses? Or had Intus really dragged me down to Impland to teach me the joys of parenting? If so, she had a messed-up way of doing it, but I expected nothing less.

What crowded my mind, overriding all other concerns, was the image of Kate and Mithnite sitting in our kitchen, looking stressed and with no idea what had happened. Kate was used to me disappearing on jobs, and I'd done it since coming back into the Hidden world, but had checked in as regularly as possible. And besides, she'd been involved in quite a lot of what had gone on.

I needed to get in touch, give her a call, but knew now wasn't the time. Damn, I didn't even have a cell phone on me, hadn't used one for days as far as I could recall. No, wait, had I picked it up when I got dressed before going to Council HQ and all this nonsense began?

I checked my pockets, relieved to discover the hard lump that meant I wasn't cut off from Kate. I fished it out carefully, gripping Dancer around the waist tightly with one hand.

Damn, utterly trashed. It was hardly surprising, but I knew we had to get to a phone. Were there phone booths these days? I couldn't think when I'd last seen one, but I hadn't been looking. I pocketed the phone—never litter—and held on tight as Dancer sped up on a straight.

Some time later, I became vaguely aware of the change in the noise of the engine and the steady vibration between my legs. We were slowing. Dancer turned to get my attention, then pointed ahead.

A car and a large black van with tinted windows, proper gangster style, blocked the narrow road ahead, no way for us to get around them.

The bike slowed further, crawling forward now. I glanced behind and tapped Dancer on the shoulder. He took a look then nodded. We were trapped. Cars approached from the rear—we would have to fight.

I hopped off as Dancer stopped and flicked out the kickstand. He shut the bike down, which I thought showed real cool—a sign he was confident he wouldn't have to ride off in a hurry—and we waited.

"You look awful," I said, noting the black spider's web of marks all over his bitten forearm, spreading up under his rolled up sleeve.

"You too," he said, although I wasn't sure if he meant in general or if I was looking suitably zombieish. Probably a little of both.

We stood and waited, the Romanians taking their time to come close from behind. Cautious, as they didn't know what we could do.

"Wish we had another gun. One with bullets," I added needlessly.

"Yeah, but it was risky. Could have lost an arm."

"True," I agreed. I inspected the bike for the first time, wondering about what Ethelbald had said regarding the modifications he'd seemed inordinately proud of. I'd seen his bikes before, rode a few over the years, and he always liked to surprise his customers with something that blew them away—after all, they paid a lot for his work. It was what he was known for, and he had a reputation to maintain.

I ran my eyes over the beautiful, gleaming body, and noted some of the strange protrusions that were clearly detachable. Weapons of a very shiny, chromed variety. I yanked on a bulbous ball of polished metal only to find it came away with a chain attached and a handle that slid out of a tube running along the rear, part of the grip for a passenger.

"For you, Boss." I handed it to Dancer and he looked at me, surprised. "Ah, you've never seen this kind of work before, right?"

"Nope. But I'm sure glad you have."

I fumbled about, checking quickly, knowing the wyrmlings might attack at any moment. My eyes caught on a cross shape with a simple pattern, and I gripped it and yanked hard.

Schlick.

"Sweet. Remind you of anything?" I asked Dancer as I swished the sword left then right.

"Hell, he really does take his work seriously."

"He's an artist," I said. "Hey, you got a phone? I think maybe I should call Kate."

"Sure, it's in my... Damn, I left my jacket, and it was in there."

"It's okay, I'm sure we'll be fine," I said, feeling quietly confident despite the tiredness and the you-know-what on the old leg.

We held ourselves tall and proud despite the hurt. The cars behind came to a stop, and they too turned off their engines.

All was quiet for a moment, so welcome after the constant sounds of engines and the wind roaring in my ears. A man emerged from the passenger's side of the van up ahead and moved to the side. Without looking at us, he slid open the door.

Dancer and I looked at each other, checking we were up for whatever they threw at us.

We weren't. We were wrecks. "Let's give it our best shot," he said, squaring his shoulders and swinging the shiny weapon.

"Wouldn't have it any other way." I adjusted my grip on the sword, took what I thought was a suitably kick-ass looking stance, and got ready.

Then the zombies shuffled out of the van and I may have panicked, just a little.

Let's Fight

"You know I'm going to slap you across the head if we get out of this alive, right?"

"Yeah, I know." Dancer sighed and rubbed at his temple like he was getting ready for the blow. This wasn't just about Dragon and what we'd done to him. These were the wyrmlings that had rushed over from Romania not only to meet the man they adored, but to kill the one they despised.

"Just what the hell did you do to these guys?"

"I told you. I maimed about forty of them and killed a few more."

"But why?"

"Spark, there isn't time. Later, okay?"

"Damn straight, later."

We watched as the driver got out and then the car beside the van emptied of men, five in all. All looking powerful, all looking angry, all looking huge.

Not stupid, though. They waited until the zombies were closer to us than to them before exiting the vehicles, and, needless to say, those behind us were now heading straight for us.

Time for action.

I sank deep into dark magic enforcer mode, tattoos bursting, magic whirling, eyes black as Dancer's hair and my rage. I sent out feelers toward the men and picked up on their vibrations. Only two were channeling the Empty, the rest were just followers of Dragon. Shifters, not a one of them a simple, Regular guy. Made sense. Wyrmlings were all about magic and the man behind it all, and I knew now wasn't the time to remind them he was a nasty bugger and had lied about being the father of all shifters.

The men all held back, smiling viciously, ready to watch the show.

"You brain 'em, I'll chop off their heads," I said staring straight ahead, not in the mood for any more nasty surprises.

"Deal." Dancer grimaced as he swapped the mace from right to left then moved it back to his right. If he felt anything like me, then the limb was burning and aching so bad he felt like asking me to hack it off. Or maybe it was just me being a lightweight about an ickle zombie nibble.

"Oh, no, wait. Hey, maybe they won't attack as we're turning into one of them," I suggested hopefully.

I was wrong, because the zombies, pretty well-preserved ones at that, sped up and did the old arms flailing and teeth gnashing that they are so well known for.

Dancer roared and ran at them, so I did likewise, not wanting to be left out of all the fun—not. He swung and connected with the lead zombie, smashing half its face away. I was about to finish it off but realized there was no point, its brains were already spilling over the road.

I swung out hard at those to my right, aiming high and getting a good clean draw across two necks but missing the third. They dropped and I stabbed down hard at first one then the other, right through the skull. The third came at me fast, and I only just managed to sidestep as it clawed at my face.

Spinning, I jabbed the hilt into an eye and as it staggered backward I faced it and thrust expensive steel hard and fast right through its throat. The zombie fell forward onto the sword, right up close, and its weight almost toppled me. I yanked down and away, retrieved the blade, and staggered to the side as two more came in fast, moaning and with only one thing on their minds.

With the blade down low, I swung to my right, backhanding like I was returning a volley, and chopped through their knees. They ignored it, felt no pain, but I'd obviously severed something. They collapsed as they tried to move, legs angling in all the wrong directions, bones crunching as they were mangled under the weight of their own bodies.

Again, I punctured their throats, the zombie preservative that stopped them rotting within a few weeks of being infected leaking out in lumpy, dirty brown puddles around both bodies.

Arms already exhausted, I took a deep breath and willed magic into my limbs to keep me going, knowing that without it I'd be getting my second zombie bite of the day.

Turning to help Dancer, knowing he'd be in bad shape, I stopped with my arm half-raised.

"Wow, nice going, dude." I stared at the bodies on the patchy road. Each of them leaking, heads smashed and all the stuff that's meant to be inside now very much not.

"Thanks. Told you I could fight when needed."

"I never doubted it," I said, trying to sound convincing. It was stupid, but I still found it hard to shake the image of the man he'd portrayed, where he never showed he could fight and stuck strictly to necromancy. I had to get over it. This was the true Dancer, and he was formidable, if still an utter muppet.

The wyrmlings were chattering loudly, gesticulating at us and goading each other. "You know what they're saying?" I asked.

"Yeah. They're saying they aren't happy and they want us dead."

"I kind of guessed that much."

"You asked."

"You ready?"

"Nope. You?"

"Absolutely not, but let's do it, anyway. I'll deal with the wizards, you deal with the shifters."

Dancer turned and stared at me hard. "What? That hardly seems fair."

"Fine. Whatever. You do the wizards, I'll take the shifters."

"No, wait. Hang on. Um..." Dancer weighed up the pros and cons of each, and while he wasted time the wyrmlings attacked.

"I'm definitely gonna slap you for this," I warned.

"I think I deserve it," Dancer moaned.

As they closed in, I heard the sound of a vehicle behind us, but didn't bother turning. We had enough to deal with already, me getting more worried would have to wait awhile.

Feeling Sleepy

As I focused my will into my hands, ready to blast until I dropped, a terrible lethargy took hold and I swear I almost lay down and went to sleep right there and then. I was beyond tired, beyond spent, this was something else.

This was the sleep of the zombie.

Some infected turn almost immediately. The virus enters their system and that's it—undead. But for Hidden it's different, and it can creep up on you in many ways. The end result is always the same, although the path you take to get there can vary wildly.

Not only that, but once true zombie some manage to maintain their sense of self for many years. Sure, they have the cravings, but if they can be satisfied then many zombies can act rationally, even hold conversations and wax lyrical about the benefits of undead immortality. Others sink fast into utter madness, watching from behind a veil, unable to halt the infection from overwhelming them completely. They cannot control limbs or cravings, are lost to themselves as they sink further and further from their humanity until all that remains is the shell. Their soul no longer truly here, or free to move on to the next realm. Limbo of the worst kind.

One thing that was the same for them all was that there was no turning back, and no way they could ever be allowed to be part of the general population. Urges were unstoppable, actions wild and often came seemingly out of nowhere, and day by day they rotted away, slowly or rapidly depending on the expertise of those that basically embalmed them to keep them from falling to bits.

Oh, and as the infection gathers pace, it springs suddenly, overwhelming you with a tiredness as it shuts you down, forcing you into slumber. A sleep many never wake from as a human being.

So I fought it, dismissed it as not even a possibility. No way was this thing gonna win. Not now, not ever.

"I hope this bloody..." my words trailed off as I turned to Dancer. He was rocking back and forth, eyes closed, mouth opening ready to release a snore.

I shook him hard and gave him the early slap he deserved. His eyes snapped open and he shuddered violently then said, "Thanks."

"My pleasure. Any time. To business?"

"Sure, let's do it."

I sank deep once more, ignored the lack of the flow in my leg where magic bottlenecked then pushed on through the broken ink on my thigh. Feeding my body and reversing some of the effects of the bite as it gained power and strength. I watched our attackers with black, Hidden eyes.

Not too powerful, and nothing I couldn't handle. As the wizards raised their hands to attack us I emptied my belly, created a vacuum, then breathed in deep and hard as I ran at the men. They faltered and stepped back, the loss of magic coming as a surprise. Guess maybe they didn't have someone like me back home and hadn't heard what I was capable of.

Good. We had surprise on our side.

Their magic came to me in great lungfuls of power. Their loss was my temporary gain and with each breath in I took more of their power and each exhalation gave most of it back to the Empty, but not all. I was growing stronger, channeling their magic into my ability to devour theirs. They shrank, becoming less of themselves.

But I couldn't focus on them all, knew that to take the innate shifter ability was a different matter entirely, so Dancer had his hands extremely full. I had no time to look behind to see what the newcomers were doing, just hoped that Dancer was on the ball now and could cope, if just for a while as I took more and more from the wizards.

They crumpled with moans and stuttering magic that shot from their hands but never reached its intended mark. I was something different now, stronger than ever and part of that was the rage inside. These men were responsible. Followers of Dragon unleashing the undead on us and look what had happened. My beautiful life ruined unless Dancer had a miracle up his bloody sleeve.

Soon their magic was gone and I breathed out with a cough, twisted ephemeral lumps of magic hissing and spitting in anger as it dissolved in the half-light and became pure again, back where it belonged.

Half a dozen magic adepts lay in various states of ruination on the pitted asphalt, features shadowed as the evening closed in, eyes sunken and cheekbones sharp, faces little more than thin skin stretched over bone.

They moaned and wailed in their mother tongue. Shamed, bereft, already hitting the terrible comedown from loss of their magical abilities. It would only get worse, not better. They were in for days, weeks, maybe months of terrible pain as their bodies called for magic they could no longer gorge on, my skills meaning they would be lucky if they ever managed to use magic again in their lives.

I left them to their pain, and moved to help Dancer. He looked like he needed it.

Like a Zoo

I tightened my grip on the sword's hilt and bellowed like I was defending against marauding invaders on the shores of my own country, ready to crush those that came to take what was mine. Which, I guess, was close to the mark.

As Dancer swung his mace at what I'm sure was a supposedly extinct wolf breed, and it cracked loudly as he made contact, a damn donkey neighed loudly, yellow teeth looking gross but dangerous nonetheless, and ran right at him. Donkeys may look cute with their big ears and adorable faces, but not when they are heading right for you—they can trample you to death no problem, kill you with a kick of a leg.

Preoccupied, he was oblivious, even to my shouted warning, so I lunged for him and tackled him to the side.

We ended up in the verge, a tangle of limbs, but I was up fast and hauled him to his feet. "Stay focused," I warned, but I could see he was almost beat, hardly anything left for him to draw on to finish this fight.

To the side of the shifters now, we finally got the chance to see how many were behind us.

It wasn't what I expected at all.

"Kate?" I called. "Mithnite? Persimmon? What the hell are you all doing here?"

"We came to help," said Persimmon as she backhanded a German Shepherd without even looking, sending it flying across the road. Damn, but she's strong.

Speaking of strong. Kate did the vampire shimmer shuffle and was at the neck of a man as surprised as me to see her. But she didn't bite, had a thing about doing it in company, and slammed his head down into asphalt instead. This was no ordinary whack, though, this had all the power of the vampire behind it, and he was dead —what with the fact his head was sunk deep into the road and all.

Mithnite was surrounded by a haze of orange, wisps of magic crackling as he called forth for more power and the Empty obliged. He tried first one way then the other, his arm shooting out at men one by one in accusation, deadly shards of magic sometimes missing their mark, but hitting eventually.

Then his power faded and he collapsed, puking up his guts, moaning and screaming as he crumpled and the price was paid for taking what wasn't his. Been there, done that, don't fancy going back one bit.

A bear roared, rising onto hind legs. It was at least seven feet tall and definitely not after marmalade sandwiches. The massive creature cut across the road in a second, surprisingly fast for such a huge beast.

Dancer, unbelievably, stepped in front of me and swung in what seemed like a lazy arc with his good hand, the mace shining like gleaming armor as the headlights of Kate's vehicle caught the chrome.

Somehow, maybe through expert timing, or utter luck, the mace connected with the head of the bear at exactly the right moment.

It slammed sideways and time sped up again. As it stirred, and clawed at the road, finding purchase and was up and ready for more, I felt a welcome circling motion on my chest as magic swirled faster and faster, gathering power and forming what I had in mind before it shot down my arm and spat out my palm as a bulbous lump of death.

It tore through the thick neck of the bear and as it fell for the last time it returned to the form of a man. A hairy lump of a guy who clearly enjoyed eating pies and wasn't averse to seconds.

On high alert, emotions fighting between happiness at seeing everyone, and annoyance that they'd put themselves in harm's way and were an added responsibility, I scanned for more wyrmlings.

One left.

Just Us

We rushed over to everyone and I hugged Kate tight. Boy did it feel good. The warmth, the smell of her hair, the familiarity of her body. The stuff of dreams. "What are you doing here?" I whispered into her ear.

"Persimmon came and said she thought something was up with you guys. That we should come look for you. That maybe you needed help. Looks like you did." Kate pulled back a little and studied me. I guess I didn't look too pleasant judging by the look of concern on her face.

"Faz, what's going on?"

"Later," I said, turning as the large dog, some kind of mongrel, padded carefully toward us all.

"Persimmon, you didn't have to come, we're fine."

"Yeah, right, looks like it," she said, shrugging her shoulders.

"I think it's a very nice thought," said Dancer, trying to smile at Persimmon but she just looked at him in concern.

"Don't worry, he always looks like he's about to pass a brick when he tries to smile," I told her. "You'll get used to it."

"Spark! I do not."

"Um, you kinda do, Dancer," said Kate, her breezy confidence more welcome by the minute.

"Shut up," he mumbled, but at least he stopped with the grimacing. Hell, if I'd thought he looked bad before, he looked positively half-dead now, which I guess he was. Guess we both were.

The dog stopped and sniffed a corpse then moved forward cautiously. He stopped at what I guess he assumed was a safe distance—it wasn't—then morphed back into human form. He stood, naked and confident in front of us all. He had long, dry hair as wild as the look in his eyes. This dude really wanted to see us dead. Dancer, anyway.

"You stole. You must die," said the shifter, squaring his shoulders, accent so strong it was almost unintelligible.

"What did you steal?" I asked Dancer, but before I got an answer the man shifted again.

Persimmon leapt at him.

It was over before it even began. She ripped out his throat mid-air and landed on top of his body, ready for more. He was already dead.

She stood tall as she stepped off him. Her body gleamed like an idealized statue carved by the hand of God, illuminated by the car's headlights. Mute, we all just stared at her.

"Um, I think you have some explaining to do, Dancer," I said, turning to him before Kate caught me looking and decided she'd very much like to rip my throat out in a similar fashion to Persimmon's victim.

Dancer was lost to his dreams, eyes glued to Persimmon like strings were connected from his visual cortex to her bouncy bits.

Mithnite coughed and managed to get to his feet. I don't think it was only because of the naked, stupendous body in front of him, but I'm sure it helped him recover faster than he would have otherwise.

"Dancer! Hello?" I got up in his face and he snapped out of it. Reluctantly.

"Huh?"

"I said, you've got some explaining to do."

Persimmon walked past and said, "Dick," to Dancer, but I caught a quiver of a lip, maybe the hint of a smile. There was no longer any doubt in my mind. I was sure she had a soft spot for him. Was she showing off? If so, then wow, this was one brazen, tough woman.

She moved back to where she'd sensibly taken off her clothes before springing into action, and Kate held them up for her, not without managing a good deal of frowning at Mithnite and Dancer. I was getting off lightly for being a good boy.

"You should wear dresses," suggested Kate. "It's quicker to get undressed and if you have to shift quickly it won't hurt as the material splits."

"Tried it," grunted Persimmon as she slipped into jeans so tight you'd think she'd need a special machine to get into them. "Don't like 'em."

Kate handed her her vest and Persimmon took it, thanking her. "Oh." Kate studied Persimmon as she dressed. They hadn't spoken much, this trip probably being the first time, but they seemed relaxed with each other, which was good. I'd got into a little trouble in the past because of Persimmon, and the last thing I wanted was them at each other's throats. You've seen how that goes down. It ain't a metaphor I'm using here.

There's something very sexy about a woman stretching up and slipping a tight vest over an ample bosom. Um, yeah, not that I was looking or anything. The other guys were, but not me. Kate glanced my way and I was brushing at my suit—come on, give me a break, I'd had a hard day and women kept getting naked lately. It was becoming distracting and Mithnite was in for a serious letdown as at this rate he'd expect to see gorgeous flesh every time he walked out the door.

When I was his age what I wouldn't have given for all these bodies to be on show, plus he had a fortune in gold and he'd only been with me a few days. It took me a hundred years to get this far and he had it within hours.

I put an arm around Mithnite and then used a finger to close his jaw and turn his head away from Persimmon. "Nice to see you, buddy. Thanks for helping."

"My pleasure. You look like crap, Spark. What's this about?"

"Tell you later, okay?" He nodded. "But let me give you some advice. Don't go ogling the ladies. They don't like it. And in our world it's liable to get you very dead, very quick. Persimmon's a nice woman, and I know she's hot, but don't stare."

Mithnite flushed but said, "Okay, sorry. It's just, well, everyone keeps losing their clothes lately, me too. Is it always like this?"

"No. You just caught us all at a weird time in our lives, I guess. Normally, you stay dressed and get covered in goop. You'll find that you spend a lot of cash on clothes, as they always get ripped."

Without thinking, I looked down at my suit and poked the large flap of material by my thigh. Mithnite followed my gaze and then asked, way too loud, "Is that a bite mark? It looks like a human bite mark. Have you been bitten by a person?"

You know those moments when it seems like the world has somehow become devoid of sound? When all you hear is the blood pounding in your ears and you know you'll have to talk about things you really don't want to?

Yup, definitely one of those moments.

"Idiot," I said to Mithnite, before turning to face the music.

Some Explaining to Do

"Faz, what's happening? Let me see." Kate's jaw clenched and her hands bunched in fists so tight her knuckles were bone-white as she walked over slowly. She seemed to take forever.

I glowered at Mithnite and he shrugged an apology. A plethora of emotions crossed his face. From confusion, to worry he was in trouble with me, to concern when he saw Kate's rigid body. Understanding dawned as he studied the bite mark, visible for all to see now I was no longer trying to hide it.

There was no point. It was time to explain to my friends and family what was going on.

Kate came close and I lifted my gaze from my leg to meet her eyes. They were wet, but she refused to let the tears run freely. Brave woman. My woman. My anchor in the storm of this often sad life. I didn't want this. I wanted to be happy, to live forever with this beautiful, strong, proud, caring, also-infected woman. Damn! What curses we had laid at our door. Her a vampire, and now this. She was coping, with a few hiccups, sure, but this was different and everyone in our world knew it.

You don't get to live your life how you want when one of the walking dead. You get locked away from the world and grow cold and obsessed with the sparks of life signaling sentience that are constantly firing within the human brain.

Yum. Brains.

I've often pondered the true reason why the undead crave human flesh, specifically brains, and I'm sure I have the answer now. It's the seat of all human emotion, all reasoning, all life. Synapses fire and send a barrage of electrical impulses all over this three pound lump we each have in our skull. It's like magic only more esoteric, more unknowable.

Such a wondrous and fascinating thing the brain is. Millions of little pulses of electricity that are translated into feeling, thought, raw emotion. Pleasure, pain, happiness, and unbearable grief, all from little bursts of energy that come as if from nowhere and then are gone in a moment. Giving rise to all we know, understand, crave, desire, and abhor. The very basis for our lives.

Now that's real magic, the true mystery of the cosmos.

Zombies crave this energy, this wondrous magic. The only one they have a hope of gaining access to. They want to consume the essence of a person, devour a lifetime's worth of memories, emotions, thoughts and pain in a few blissful moments. They *need* magic of the most potent kind. And maybe, just maybe, there's an answer to the workings of the human mind buried deep down inside the infection that drives them to such mindless greed, such obsessive cravings for what makes a human being tick.

That's all well and good, and something to ponder when time permits, but right here in the middle of the road surrounded by dead men, dead dreams, and dead desires, all I could think was that it wasn't fair.

"I'm sorry," was all I could manage as Kate checked me over, eyes coming to rest on my leg.

"Oh, Faz." Kate hugged me tight and I felt the tears rather than heard her crying.

She stayed like that for a while, just gripping the back of my jacket in tight bunches, and it broke my heart. We'd come so close. Things were finally good, no, great for us. We had welcomed Mithnite into our home and we had a few friends—okay, maybe one or two—and now it was all going to shit.

Something snapped in my head and I eased her off and held her at arm's length.

"I'll beat it. Dancer and I will beat this thing. No way are we gonna be—"

"Dancer, too?" asked Kate in shock. Persimmon and Mithnite gasped as attention turned to the Head of the UK Hidden Council. Our friend, my boss, Mr. Strange himself.

"Damn, sorry, dude. It's getting rather emotional."

"Don't sweat it," he said with a resigned shrug. He rolled up sleeves he'd hastily pulled down when they arrived and they inspected the bite on his left forearm.

It was hard to make it out with the shadows we all cast, but it looked a hell of a lot worse. The dark spider's web of infection was thicker and blacker than ever and the skin looked ready to split. It was grossly swollen and discolored and had spread up his arm.

"What happened?" asked Kate, still in the dark about a lot of what had gone on. Maybe Persimmon had filled her in on events at Council HQ but there would be a lot she was unaware of.

"We got bit by zombies. We saved most of our people when Dragon attacked, and that's all done with now, but, well, we got bitten. Um, I said that, right?" I was losing it a little. Trying to remain calm and unaffected but knew I was failing, badly.

"You should have come home," said Kate, squeezing my hand tight. I hadn't even realized she'd taken it.

"We were kind of busy running away from the wyrmlings. Dancer here is pretty unpopular with the Romanian faction, and still has some explaining to do about that," I said, giving him the daggers but my heart wasn't in it.

"Sorry, okay? I'll tell you guys all about it. Look, let's get out of here. It's a bloody mess here and a quiet road, but we need to deal with these bodies and get safe. Kate, you got a phone I can borrow?"

"Sure." Kate fished out a phone from her jacket pocket, a green three-quarter length leather number that was damn stylish.

"Hey, is that new?" I asked.

"No, I got it ages ago. You already said you liked it."

"Oh, oops. Well, I do, and it suits you. Brings out the color of your hair." Her brown-blond hair was shades lighter against the green, and it made her blue eyes all the more deep and soulful. Her full lips, always a strong feature, seemed redder and more luscious. Maybe I was just taking her in while I still could, or maybe I'd finally stopped to take the time to admire her after the years I was lost to myself, battling inner demons and neglecting her while I wallowed and refused my destiny.

"Can you beat this? Is there a cure?" she asked, forgiving me for the oversight regards her clothes.

"Dancer says there is. That's where we're headed. To see someone he says can help."

"Oh. Let's go, then."

"How long you got left?" asked Persimmon.

"I don't know. A day. Less."

Kate gasped, Mithnite stared at the road and shuffled his feet, and Persimmon held my gaze and said, "Shit, sorry. That really sucks."

"Yeah, tell me about it."

Dancer came back into the glare of the headlights from the darkness where he'd made a call. "Okay, someone will be here soon. We'll put the bodies in the van and the rest will be taken care of. Let's move it, people. If anyone comes by, we're in a world of trouble and we don't have time for it now."

It was a relief to be hauling dead wizards and shifters down the road and manhandling them into the van, which says how much I wanted to avoid talking about our current zombification.

A few minutes later we were done, and with the vehicles parked up at the roadside we held our collective breath as a few cars came down the road and pulled up. The lead driver got out and went straight to Dancer, ignoring the rest of us. After a quick conversation, he signaled to the other vehicles and four men got out of the cars.

A minute later we were standing beside a clear road as if nothing had happened.

"Okay, let's go somewhere quiet and have a quick rest, then we'll go sort ourselves out and we'll be good as new," I said, trying to convince myself and everyone else I was telling the truth.

I knew I wasn't. I suspected Dancer had been lying all along. That this was his way of getting us as far away as possible from those we loved and cared about. That he knew the infection would take us soon but at least we'd be unable to hurt those we wanted to protect the most.

He may be a muppet, but he's got a heart of gold. And soon it would stop beating.

A Rubbish Dinner

The sight of ourselves in the stark light of the mirrors came as a shock. We looked truly awful. The infection had spread. Creeping from the wounds, black tendrils crawled across our skin and out in every direction. As we gawped at each other in shock and not a little disgust, full of despair verging on desperation with our shirts unbuttoned and trousers around our ankles in a restroom in a dodgy service station, we looked like we were into some serious fetish stuff. Anyone that had come in would have run a mile when they saw the state of us.

The spreading infection was stark against Dancer's skin. Mine mingled with my ink until it was hard to tell what was what. I was now almost black all over. Our flesh was mottled, discolored and all kinds of nasty. It had begun to crack as though we'd dried up after being out in the sun, like old leather hides in serious need of oil.

But oil wouldn't solve our problem, only strong magic of a very specific kind could save us now. It all came down to Dancer and the contact he was still being coy about.

"This is so messed up," I said staring at our reflection. Our faces were the worst—like we'd gone ten rounds with someone twice our size and had lost every one. Black and blue and nasty, dark veins crawling up our necks and mottling our cheeks like every blood vessel was corrupted with poison, which is exactly what they were. We finished cleaning up and did our best to look respectable but failed miserably. We left the restroom without saying another word.

We went to join the others in the empty, odd smelling service station eatery.

*

"That was, without doubt, the worst thing I have ever eaten in my entire life. And I've eaten a lot of weird stuff." Dancer placed his cutlery down on his plate neatly—his empty plate—and sat back with a frown of accusation.

"So why did you eat it?" I asked, even though my plate was clear, too.

"I was hungry," he said, matter-of-fact.

"Fair enough."

"Guys, can we stop talking about the crap bloody dinner and talk about what's important?" said Mithnite, sounding more mature than I'd ever heard him.

"Sorry, you're right. Damn, I don't know what to say. Look, this sucks, and I know you're all worried. It's why we didn't tell you, um, and we didn't have a phone. And we were being chased."

"Excuses," said Persimmon.

"Hey, this is your fault," I said, getting angry for no reason.

"I was worried," she said, and that meant a lot.

"I know. I'm sorry. Persimmon, thanks for looking out for us, and you guys helped a lot back there. But you all need to go home. We have to deal with this alone. Just us guys."

"So I can come?" asked Mithnite, clearly not wanting to leave.

"No, dude. I meant Dancer and me. You all need to leave."

"No." Kate pushed her plate of untouched food away and dared me to defy her.

"Kate, I—"

"Just don't even go there, Faz. I said no."

"If I may?" said Dancer, nervously putting a hand through his hair.

"Be my guest," said Kate, looking like she'd burst into tears again.

"This person who I think can help, she's, er, someone I've been in touch with for a few years. I can't tell you anything much about her, only that she came out of the blue and it was a real surprise. She's powerful, knows about things none of us do, and, well —"

"Just get on with it," snapped Kate. "Sorry, sorry, this is too much to take in. How can you both stand it?"

"Because we have no choice, love," I said, but wondering the same thing. It felt ridiculous to be sitting there huddled around a dirty Formica table somewhere on the outskirts of Birmingham when we should have been on the move, never stopping until we got wherever we were going.

"Okay, look. I told Spark this and now I'll tell you all. I can't talk about this woman. If I do, she'll know, and she's a little, shall we say, protective of her privacy. She gets jumpy, will be impossible to find if she thinks someone is looking for her. That's how she lives, how she always has, apparently, and I'm not about to risk it."

"But she can cure you guys?" asked Persimmon.

"Yes, she can. Or, at least I think she can. I've met her once and there's an agreement between us that I wouldn't talk of her to anyone until she decided the time was right. I don't even know if she'll agree to see us. But if she does, you have to know it won't be an easy meeting. There are things I can't tell you and I'm sorry, but there we are."

"Damn, Dancer, you're being way too mysterious about this woman. Why did she come to you?"

"I can't say. She was looking for something but when she came she decided it wasn't the right time and she left. But she can help, I'm sure. That's all you need to know. She's our last, our only, chance, and I don't want to blow this."

"So let's go," said Kate.

"Yeah, we need to sort you out before it gets worse. You have seen yourselves, right?" said Mithnite dragging Kate's plate over and tucking in. He was a growing lad and seemingly devoid of taste buds. Dancer and I had eaten because we were so starved from this infection, and even then we struggled. Mithnite seemed to actually enjoy the overpriced food.

"We have, more's the pity," I said, staring in wonder as he downed the lumpy, cold mashed potato with relish and bit off half a sausage I was sure contained less meat than was legal.

"So, let's do this thing."

"Dancer?" I asked.

"Fine, you can all come. But Spark and I go in alone. You wait well away and you do not, under any circumstances, come try to find us once we leave you for the final part of this journey. If you agree to that, and this is an order coming from your Head, then you can tag along until then. This is serious. We may not even make it to the end, and if we turn before we do then you have to do what's necessary. Am I making myself clear here?" Dancer made eye contact with everyone in turn, showing a side of him we don't often see. He was in charge. To be respected. To be obeyed.

There were murmurs of agreement and I knew it broke Kate's heart to think that this could be the end of our life together.

"Kate, you have to say you will. I refuse to be kept going if this thing wins. You have to say you'll end it if it comes to that."

"I won't let either of you be a zombie. Haha, that sounds so stupid," she said, words coming out imbued with infinite sadness, tinged with lost dreams of a happy future that could go on indefinitely.

"So, let's go," said Dancer. He stood and Mithnite stuffed the last sausage into his mouth while we all stared at him.

"What? I was hungry."

The word brains crowded my mind and I almost said it out loud. A strange feeling overtook me and I lost all emotion. For a brief moment all I saw were sparks of energy in three heads. More than anything, I wanted to smash them open and scoop out what was hidden inside.

I turned to Dancer and a look passed between us that told us both we'd experienced something similar.

"Definitely time to go. And let's be quick," I said.

Dancer nodded.

We were close to running out of time now.

"Brains," I whispered, and slammed my hand over my mouth. Nobody noticed apart from Dancer.

He had an unnerving glint in his eye.

Heading North

I missed Cardiff. I missed the manageable scale of the city with its easy driving and laid-back attitude. I missed my home, Grandma—hell, she'd freak if she knew about this—Madge's more than ever after the gross meal I'd just eaten, and the sense of familiarity above all else.

Coasting along motorways, heading north to an unknown destination, everything was in free fall. Landmarks were if not alien then unfamiliar. Sure, I'd traveled extensively, but the majority of my time was spent at the heart of all things magical, and that meant Cardiff. With its signs in both Welsh and English, its mix of people and cultures, the bay, the shopping district that was so small compared to other cities it hardly even qualified, but it was where I lived. Home.

All these roads, the never-ending concrete and bridges, everyone in a hurry, roadworks and endless traffic jams and coned lanes that went on for miles where nobody seemed to be doing any work to warrant the interruption, it was all maddening. Frightening, too, in a way.

Where was everyone going? What was the rush? Why was everything in a constant state of disrepair. I felt insular, like I'd ignored the wider world, had blinkers on. Maybe I had, but it was from choice. I don't like travel, dislike interruptions to my focus or my work.

And I abhor being a passenger when Kate drives.

Mithnite was in the back, a stream of consciousness spewing from his mouth like he was trying to empty out all the words he knew and wasn't overly concerned about the order. I understood. It had been a helluva day. Damn, earlier we'd dropped into the dragon's lair and now here we were, the same day, so much having changed it made your head spin.

Kate was driving like a maniac as she tried to keep up with Dancer and Persimmon. Cars flashed by as we sped through the dark evening, feeling like we were on another planet when sections of road were devoid of streetlights as part of the government's cut down on the exorbitant cost of lighting the country. It was a good idea, but it was eerie when the road was empty of other cars and we were hemmed in by high banks.

We were the last people on earth. Hurtling toward oblivion mere feet from death if a simple miscalculation sent the car out of control.

I repeatedly pushed my foot on an imaginary brake, nerves already shot without this additional stress.

"Guys, I need to say something."

"Don't, Faz. Just don't, okay?" Kate glanced at me, knowing I was about to get maudlin.

"I'm sorry, but I need to. Mithnite?"

"Yeah?" He leaned forward between the front seats with a sympathetic look I hated as I knew it meant I wasn't being seen as me, but as a victim.

I refused to be a victim, and was why I didn't want to tell them. I'd seen it enough over the years, had done it myself, and it brought back bad memories of the worst kind. When people know you have an illness that's what they see. Not the real you, the person you are, but something else. A victim. Their vision clouded with sympathy and thoughts of your end, rather than the person you are beneath the illness that becomes all-consuming not only to you but to everyone around you.

"Spark, you okay?"

"Oh, sorry, dude, just thinking. Okay, now look. I'm sorry that we've welcomed you into our little family and this has happened. I thought we'd have a long future together. That I'd be there for you and maybe help you get where you want to be in life, and for that I apologize."

"You don't have to apologize, Spark. This isn't your fault. You were saving everyone, and that's a seriously cool thing to do."

"Maybe, or maybe it was stupid. Anyway," I held up a hand so he wouldn't speak, "it is what it is. Promise me you'll look after Kate. That you'll be there when she needs you."

"Faz, I can look after myself, and you aren't going anywhere," said Kate.

"I'm just being sensible. Promise me, Mithnite."

"I promise."

All sound was sucked out the car for a moment, the pressure changed, making my ears pop, and then I felt the warm glow of anticipation. Time for some luscious lobes.

"Oi, you can't go driving this fast, it's dangerous," said the faery as she scowled at first Kate, then me, then Mithnite. "What's that?" she asked, pointing a perfect finger at my young apprentice.

"I'm, Mith... Mithnite. Ugh, I don't feel too well." Mithnite, wide-eyed and looking green, cramped up as the faery circled his head, looking bored.

"Bloody hell, this is all I need. What are you doing here?"

"Your Mithnite here made a promise, so I've come to get his signature." With that, a tiny piece of parchment appeared in her gorgeous hand and faery dust sprinkled down onto the dash as she landed in front of me and scowled. "Ooh, you look nasty. You should get some medicine for that."

"Have you got any?" I asked, my heart leaping for a moment, thinking the faery could save me.

"Nah, we don't do that sort of thing. Can't interfere, you know that. Not with stuff like this."

"Yeah, just when it suits you," I muttered.

"I heard that! Don't you get smart with me, Faz Pound. I know all about you. Everyone heard what happened with Florenta and Fabianne."

"And? They nearly got me killed," I protested, but she wasn't listening.

"Can this wait?" asked Kate. "I'm driving here."

"You don't set the rules," said the faery, indignant. She spun in a circle, her sparkling, azure dress hugging her body so tight it may as well have been sprayed on. She gave me a sly look then slowly pushed her hair behind an ear and I swear she angled her head a little to better catch the light from the glowing dashboard.

I swallowed and tried to think unsexy thoughts, but damn she had some seriously awesome lobes. So perfect. So tiny and yummy and utterly desirable.

Lickable.

"Wow, your ears are awesome," said Mithnite as he craned forward, the sickness at encountering a faery, probably for the first time, having passed a lot faster than I'd expected.

"What, these plain old things?" she said, exposing the other one and turning side to side.

"Oh, yeah. Can I touch them?" asked Mithnite, reaching forward before I could stop him.

"No you may not!" The faery flew close to Mithnite, her deadly, razor sharp wings mere millimeters from his nose. Mithnite hardly reacted at all, just kept staring.

She turned to me and flew back in front. "Is he simple? Why isn't he scared?"

"I don't think he knows about the wings," I said wishing she'd just go away.

"Well he should. Now, I'm busy, sign here." She thrust the contract out to Mithnite and a tiny quill appeared in her other hand.

"What's that?" asked Mithnite, squinting as he peered at the miniature print.

"Damn, sorry, dude. Um, you made a promise, so you..." Something wasn't right. "Hey, hang on. You only have to sign to say you'll stick to your promise if it's made to true Hidden or true Hidden make it. We are neither of those things."

"What's wrong with you people? Ugh, humans. You're both true Hidden, or are now, anyway. You, Faz Pound, are Hidden, because of the incident with Reade Littlejohn. Which us fae will never forget, I might add."

"None of that was my fault," I said, but she didn't care. "You said we're both Hidden, true Hidden? He's a wizard, not a true magical creature."

"I haven't got time for this. I'm not your bloody magic guide. Just sign it, Mithnite Soos, so I can go do something productive like wash my hair." The faery thrust out her parchment again and Mithnite looked to me.

"Better sign it, dude. But be warned, you made a promise and now you're making it official. You have to look out for Kate like you promised, or there will be consequences."

"I said I would, didn't I?" moaned Mithnite, totally out of his depth.

"Yes, you did. But just so you know."

"Jeez, hurry up, hurry up. Look, young 'un, if you go back on your word then I'll personally wipe you from the face of this ugly earth and nobody will ever even remember you existed. Kapeesh?"

"Um, s'pose."

Mithnite took the offered quill and scrawled his name as small as possible. The faery rolled up the promise.

"Now, what's this about him being true Hidden?" I asked, but she was gone. I turned to Mithnite. He looked edgy, and not because of the faery. "Mithnite, what did she mean?"

"No idea. Honest. That was weird. Haha." He leaned back and smiled a tight smile. "I feel a little funny."

"Hang in there. Hopefully, this won't take much longer." I caught Kate's eye and she mouthed a silent, "What's he hiding?" I shook my head.

He was holding out on us, that much was clear. What did the faery mean, true Hidden? He was just a lad trying to be a proper wizard, not a supernatural being.

Right?

A Long Night

We drove through the night. I kept thinking back on what the faery had said, and my idiocy for getting caught again with the promise thing. But I hadn't thought of myself as true Hidden, and even now I'm sure it was debatable, even for the fae. No, this was something to do with Mithnite but it was obvious he didn't want to talk about it. Maybe he didn't know, maybe it was a mistake on the faery's part? It wasn't unheard of for them to break the rules or get things totally wrong. I knew that from personal experience.

But this was merely a distraction to take my mind off the problem at hand.

Several times I found myself almost asleep, my eyes closing no matter how much I fought it and no matter how often I stuck my head out the window. I explained to Kate that under no circumstances was she to allow me to sleep as if I did I might never wake up the same again. She was shocked, obviously concerned, and I caught her checking not only that I was still awake but still alive. It was past midnight and still we drove on.

The infection raged. I was burning up, so terribly hot. Like my body was taking advantage of being alive while it could and devouring fuel reserves as fast as possible. Relishing the heat before the cold of death became my only companion.

The bite mark no longer throbbed and ached, it was well beyond that now. My entire leg hurt beyond belief until I found it almost impossible to move it.

My crotch was on fire, itching like I'd caught something nasty, and my hips screamed with an intensity that made my shoulder issues feel like nothing but a minor irritation. I could feel the spread of the virus across my flesh and how it was insinuating itself deep into the very core of my being. Taking hold, weakening my immune system, making me susceptible to all manner of mild infections or germs that my body usually fought off with no problem.

Magic kept me immensely healthy when I wasn't at death's door. Meaning, I never went to the doctors or the hospital, never got a cold or the flu, and was the epitome of health even though I ate at Madge's and even used her cutlery.

Minute by minute, hour by terrible hour, I was becoming less of myself. Eaten from the inside out by a virus that to all intents and purposes had no cure. Was taking my health and my sanity along with it, consuming me because of a simple bite I should have avoided if I'd had any sense.

Breathing became difficult. My ribs ached with every inhalation and exhalation, and my fingers began to tingle like I'd sat on my hands. My legs kept going dead then returning to life with the worst case of pins and needles. Every so often I'd jolt my head and get a terrible pain shooting down from the base of my skull like when you fall asleep, your head lolls forward and you wake with a start and snap it back up.

But worst of all was that I slept, I know I did. Maybe just for a second, if that, and I'd wake instantly, freaked out. Okay, utterly terrified that I was dead and would lunge for Kate and slam her head into the steering wheel and we'd crash and I'd crawl on mangled legs to get to her and eat her while still warm.

The journey became utterly intolerable and every time my head dipped I was certain I'd closed my eyes for longer.

How was Dancer still riding his bike? How hadn't he fallen off.

I was about to say something to Kate about this when I heard a cough from the rear and turned. "Dancer, how'd you get in here?" I asked, staring at him. "Man, you look awful."

"Thanks. You too." He leaned back and sighed. Mithnite kept a close eye on him. To ensure he remained awake, I guess.

"Don't you remember, Faz?" asked Kate, looking at me with an even more worried expression than usual.

"Remember? Remember what?"

"We stopped over an hour ago. Dancer couldn't ride any more so he pulled over and Persimmon is riding the bike. She's behind us, following."

"Um, no, I don't remember." I tried to recall it but came up blank. Things were dire. If my short-term memory was going then it wouldn't be long before my whole life disappeared along with it.

"It's okay, don't worry about it," she said, voice wavering. She fixed her eyes on the road and sped up.

"Okay."

"How much further, Dancer?" she asked, glancing at him in the rearview. "Dancer?"

He took an age to answer then said, "Not long. Another thirty minutes, tops. You remember where I told you to go?"

"I remember."

Seems there had been a whole conversation I'd missed out on, too. This was becoming close. If we didn't get help soon we'd be brain munchers in a matter of hours.

"Spark?" croaked Dancer.

"Yeah, Boss?"

"If this doesn't go as planned then I'm sorry."

I shifted in my seat so I faced him, trying not to wince. "Nothing to be sorry about, buddy. We tried and that's the main thing."

"Not about the brain fetish thing. I'm sorry for... You'll see. I'm sorry."

The rest of the journey was made in silence apart from the heavy, labored breathing of the zombies-to-be and the quiet sobs of Kate.

See, this is why I hate road trips. They're depressing as hell and you never get to choose the music. Plus the only snacks were ones I really hoped I never got a taste for.

I snapped to attention as Adele blared out the CD player. "Ugh, turn it off, turn it off. You trying to make my last few minutes utter torture?"

"You fell asleep," accused Kate. "So I'm leaving it on so you'll stay awake." Kate turned it up and I squirmed in my seat as Adele sang about night falling, or something like that.

Damn, was I gonna go out listening to generic, overrated pop? What a bloody nightmare.

A Shuffle

"I don't like this," said Kate as she pulled up in a creepy alley, scaring a cat that emerged from a pile of garbage, glared at us, then was gone.

"It'll be fine," said Dancer, groaning as he opened the door and got out.

"Mithnite, give us a minute, okay, buddy?" I said, grateful the music had stopped now we were at the spot Dancer had directed Kate to.

"Sure, no problem," he said.

Before he got out I caught the look he gave Kate and the nod she gave in return. He was worried I'd turn and attack her. We all knew there wasn't much time left, that if Dancer's contact failed to come through then no way would we make it until morning.

My head was a fog of strange cravings and my life was slipping away, memories replaced with a hunger I resisted with my entire being.

I reached for Kate and she took my hand. "Look, it'll be okay. But if it isn't, if—"

"Faz, don't talk like that. You'll be fine, I know you will."

"I hope so. But just in case, if we don't come back, or if we do and we aren't successful, then know that I love you. Kate, you have made me happier than I have ever been in my entire life. I worship you, adore you, and I'm sorry it's come to this."

"Oh, Faz." Kate lunged across the gap and held me tight, hand cupping the back of my head like a newborn.

I shoved her away and it was the hardest thing I ever did in my life. She looked at me, shocked and bewildered. Anguish on her face at such a rejection.

"I'm sorry, I'm so sorry. It's too much, the scent of you. I can smell your brains. I want them, I..." I fumbled with the door handle, finally got it open, and forced limbs into action that ached so bad I honestly wasn't sure they'd work. Standing in the dark alley, I peered back in and said, "I'm sorry."

The last image I had of Kate was her beautiful face streaked with tears. Then I slammed the door shut and said to a nervous Mithnite who was beside me, ready to protect Kate, "Remember your promise. And if I don't see you again, make sure to keep up your studies." I patted him on the back then shuffled away from the car and moved down the alley to Dancer and Persimmon, both beside the bike.

"You ready?" asked Dancer.

"I'm ready."

"Good luck, guys. You're gonna need it, you know that, right?" Persimmon smiled weakly and took a step back without being consciously aware of the distance she created between us. I didn't blame her. Hell, if I could I'd move away from us.

"We know," I said. "Thanks, Persimmon. For everything."

"Maybe, if we, er..." Dancer trailed off, eyes darting anywhere but to Persimmon. "Um, maybe if I'm not a zombie we could go and, um—"

"Bloody hell, Dancer, you're minutes away from death and you can't even ask a girl out for a date?" said Persimmon with a chuckle.

"Only because you're so gorgeous. You make me nervous," he said, finally getting the courage to make eye contact. Dancer may be good as Head but he sure as hell isn't good with women. Guess he's just made that way. It was nice to see. Showed he was a genuine guy, not just cocky and full of himself.

"Me, gorgeous?" said Persimmon, brow creasing and looking genuinely surprised.

"Um, yeah. You do know you're like, ultra hot, right? More. You're bloody absolutely stunning. Plus, you have a very nice personality and a lovely smile," said Dancer hurriedly.

"Nice save, buddy," I said, smiling despite the ridiculousness of the situation.

"Me? Haha, that's very nice of you to say so."

"Wow, you really don't know how pretty you are, do you?" I was stunned. She always acted like she knew. Not in a way that made you think she believed herself better than anyone else, just a deep confidence. Happy in her own skin.

"I guess I'm okay," she said. "But lots of women are prettier. Anyway, if you were trying to ask me out then yes, I'd love to, Dancer." Persimmon stepped forward and kissed Dancer lightly on the cheek then stepped back out of arm's reach.

"Then I'll definitely beat this thing," said Dancer, a renewed sense of purpose in his voice and manner.

"Me too, just so I can see your face when you have to go through with your date," I said to Persimmon, knowing deep down that she genuinely liked him. Weird, eh? This day just got stranger and stranger. Goes to show that what you think about people is often far from the truth. You can't see what goes on in people's heads no matter how much you think you can.

"Dick," said Persimmon, and then she walked back to the car and got in the passenger's side.

The door closed and we waved into the glare of headlights then shambled down the alley. Dancer turned, I followed, and we left our friends behind, maybe for the last time.

It was just us now. Two men shuffling along the dark streets of a small town in the north of England, trying to hold on to the one thing that kept us human.

Love.

The Hunger

The town slept.

There wasn't a soul in sight as we wandered through cramped streets, poorly lit with many streetlights broken. Stores were shuttered, graffiti prevalent, and many of the dirty windows had for rent signs. The place had seen better days. Another victim of the out-of-town mega stores that left small businesses unable to compete. The shoppers couldn't really be blamed. Everyone was mindful of their cash flow and it may be a noble idea to support local businesses but when you can buy everything cheaper somewhere else then your family comes first. A real shame, and certainly not a way to keep communities alive, but there you go.

Soon we were away from the main part of the town and out into the suburban sprawl. Endless repetitions of similar houses, lacking the flourishes and the design considerations of homes built in the Victorian era. Why did everything have to look the same? Identical brick boxes with boring, well-manicured lawns, and dull, mid-range cars parked in the drives? Just people doing their best, Faz, don't judge.

The going got tough after about twenty minutes. We were slowing, the infection really taking hold now. I caught myself drooling and lost to dreams of cannibalism. Consumed by desire for warm flesh and lumpy brains scooped with relish into my gaping mouth.

I lost count of how often one of us had to stop and give ourselves a good talking to, or just shake out a limb as it had gone stone cold. Blood refusing to flow, everything shutting down little by little.

Soon we would be gone.

"Damn, what if we turn here?" I said, wheezing as I fought to get the words out. "We could go on the rampage and nobody will be able to stop us. We'll be past saving. I don't wanna be that guy, Dancer."

"You won't. If one of us dies then the other will deal with it, right?"

"Yeah, course." I knew we'd made that promise, but it would be easier said than done if we were any further down this rabbit hole. Heck, I wasn't sure I had the energy or the will to put my friend to rest if he died right now. What if he got away before I could destroy his brain and put an end to the nightmare before I too was gripped with the full effects of the virus?

"We need to hurry up. Not much further now, just a few more minutes. She better be in," he said as an afterthought, and I think we both felt the terror rise.

What if, after all this, we failed because this mystery woman happened to be away?

"You haven't called or checked or asked if she's here, have you?"

"No. I told you, she won't like this, not one bit. If I'd called, she would have said no. We're risking a lot here, Spark. For you, especially."

"What do you mean? Come on, this secrecy is stupid now. Don't you think I should know what I'm facing?"

Dancer kept moving although our pace was painfully slow. "No, because if I told you then you'd be in no state to deal with this. I'm sorry, okay?"

"You've said that already, a few times. Look, dude, I'm getting freaked out. What is this all about?"

"Spark, you just have to trust me. This isn't the way I wanted things to go down. I expected something very different, but I have no choice. I just hope she understands. I hope you do."

"Okay, buddy. If you think you're doing the right thing, whatever this is about, then I guess I trust you."

"Good, because we're here." Dancer put an arm to my shoulder and stared at me hard. "You have to stay calm. Don't overreact. Don't freak her out, and whatever you do, don't leave. You ready?"

"I guess. Haha, who am I kidding? Whoever this is, she's our last hope. This is it, Dancer. If this fails, our lives are over. This is our final destination."

"I know."

He didn't look convinced, he looked decidedly unsure of himself.

We turned as one and faced a boring looking small detached house with a tiny, utterly pointless lawn at the front and an entirely forgetful car in the drive. Curtains were drawn but a little light spilled out from a downstairs window. The living room, I assumed.

We walked up the short path to the front door, a cheap PVC and glass thing with a plain brass knocker more for decoration than anything as there was a bell.

Dancer pressed the button and I heard Jimi Hendrix play from the chimer somewhere in the hall. A light flipped on. Through the frosted glass I could just about make out a shape coming toward us.

The door opened.

"You promised me," said my wife, as she glared at Dancer. She puffed deep on her joint, turned from us, and shuffled back down the hallway.

This is It?

"What the fuck?" My head spun, my knees buckled, and if Dancer hadn't grabbed me and yanked me inside before I got my wits back I would have done a runner. Okay, I would have shambled off slowly and painfully, but you get the idea.

"I told you it wouldn't be easy. But it's not what you think. You have to trust me, Spark. This is it, the end. It's this or death. No more Kate, no more looking after Mithnite. Nothing."

"I... I don't know if I can. This can't be happening." I shook my head and slapped my temples as if it would clear the dream, the nightmare, and I'd be somewhere else. Waking up at home in bed would be ideal. But I was still there, still standing in a hallway with rough pine floorboards, prints by Robert Venosa on the walls, and paper lanterns strung up the stairs on a banister with chipped, cheap white paint.

"Just come in. I'm sorry, this is the worst possible time for this, but she can help. It's not her, Spark. It's not her. Just keep telling yourself that and you'll be all right."

"Ha, sure. Easy for you to say. She's dead, Dancer. I saw her die. I can't do this, it was so fucking hard then. I think I'm going mad."

"Come on." Dancer gripped my arm tight and pulled me forward.

"You have got to be kidding me," I moaned as I was pulled through the bead curtain and into what can only be described as hippie paradise. There were lava lamps, those weird tie-dye throws used as wall coverings, bongs and bottles and statues of Vishnu. Incense clouded the air, making it hard to breathe, and sat cross-legged on a cheap rug was the one person I knew for a fact I'd never see again in my life.

My head still spun. I was finally losing it. I grabbed for the curtain, pulling it down, beads spilling across the floor. I focused on the shining plastic, trying to gather myself, but it was too much and I couldn't cope.

"This is impossible," I moaned, too confused and emotionally charged to understand what was happening.

"Sorry, Spark, I knew this was a bad idea, but what choice did I have?" said Dancer, looking uncomfortable as a vampire at the dentist and for bloody good reason.

Somehow, I remained standing, although my legs were wobbling and it had nothing to do with the zombie inside almost ready to emerge. "Hey, Sarah." I smiled at the leggy lass, hair straight and down her backside, eyes glazed and smiling beatifically up at us.

She was utterly composed, hadn't batted a stoned eyelid at the mess I'd made or the mess I was in.

"You shouldn't be here. I'm not ready. I don't want to get in the way."

"Huh? What? I don't understand. I don't understand any of this." I turned to Dancer. "What's going on?"

"Calm down. Just breathe."

"I can't fucking breathe. My dead wife is sitting on the floor and I'm about to turn into a goddamn zombie."

"Okay, so it's not an ideal meeting," said Dancer.

"Zombies!" said the startled blast from the past as her high disappeared and she jumped to her feet.

"Brains." I clasped a hand to my mouth, the word like a mental trigger. All I could do was picture her gray matter spilled on the floor, me lapping it up. Scooping it with my blackened hands, the power and the sustenance fortifying my almost dead body. I reached out for a carved Indian table, a cheap import, but it toppled, and me along with it.

Dancer reached for me, but I heard him inhale sharply and his lungs rattled. I noted the change in his eyes as Sarah's scent reached him through the mire of incense.

He lunged for her, legs like stilts, his face waxy but criss-crossed with bulging black veins ready to burst from his skin and spurt putrid poison. A vein pulsed like a fat wiggly worm at his neck and he licked his lips, a hideous blue swollen thing of a tongue running over fat, ashen lips.

I tried to do the same, to taste the scent of fresh meat in the air, but my tongue was so engorged, my throat so raw with anticipation, that it hardly poked through my teeth now. They were furred up, all kinds of nasty, and all I could think was I wanted to split her skull open and devour her. Claw at her belly. Release the sweet sausages that were her bowels and suck on them until they were drained and I was full, satiated for just a while.

Thoughts of the past evaporated along with my sense of self. I forgot that this was the only other woman I had truly loved in my entire life. That I had spent decades living with her, laughing with her, loving her. That I'd watched her age and eventually get taken from me.

She was forty when we met, and died in her early sixties. It was the most painful six months of my entire life as I watched her fade away and turn from a buxom beauty full of the joys of life to a wasted skeleton. The chemo ate her away and the cancer finally won a battle she fought valiantly right until the end.

My beautiful Sarah. How I loved and adored this woman. I vowed never to get attached to another human being with such depth of emotion ever again. She was alive, she was young again. She was beautiful.

And I was about to smash her head in and feast on her brains.

If Dancer didn't get there first.

In the Kitchen

"Will somebody please explain what... the... fuck... is happening?" I shifted my position against the bindings that kept me sat in the chair, glancing around only to find I was in a cramped, outdated kitchen. Dancer was beside me, Sarah at the opposite end of the table closest to the door that led to the hallway. She held a knife in front of her and her hands shook almost uncontrollably.

"Don't you dare try to eat me or I'll kill you both," she warned.

"Um, Sarah, I don't know how this is happening, how you're here, but trust me, you don't want to kill us. If you do, we'll just turn all the quicker."

"He's right," agreed Dancer. "Unless you stab us in the brain."

"Shut up, you utter muppet."

"Oh, oops."

"Be quiet, both of you!" Sarah put a finger to her dimpled cheek in concentration, the mannerism so familiar, yet forgotten for over forty years, that I began to cry.

"How are you alive? I've missed you so much. You look young again. I saw you age, Sarah, saw you die. I was at your bedside. I held your hand as you passed." The tears were coming fast and strong now. I couldn't think about coming back from the brink of being a zombie, how much my body hurt, how ineffective the bindings were as I could burn through them hardly calling to the Empty. All I could think about was her. Watching her emaciated body fade away years too early until I was left alone.

"Don't call me that. You haven't told him, have you? You promised you wouldn't come, Dancer. You said you'd let me decide when the time was right, that you'd tell me when he was back how he should be. When he returned to the Hidden world."

"Sorry. Look, he is back, has accepted who he is. But things got complicated and I haven't had a chance to tell you. We got bitten. By zombies," Dancer added helpfully.

"I kinda guessed that. So, ugh, the washing line isn't gonna stop you, then?"

"Nope," said Dancer. He turned to me and said, "Spark, care to get these off us?"

"Sure. Whatever." I faded out for a moment, touching the Empty as lightly as possible until my ink flared subtly. Sparks danced off my broken body as the plastic-coated stuff melted away, dripping onto my suit. Whatever, it was ruined already. I reached out a hand

and grabbed Dancer's ties and let them melt away, too. He shook them off but we remained seated.

"Goddamn it, guess I look pretty stupid, eh?" said Sarah, putting down the knife.

"You look beautiful, Sarah," I said, wondering what I could do to stop her being afraid.

"Stop it. Stop it. Stop it. She's dead. Don't call me that. I'm Amber." She glared at Dancer. "Will you tell him, please? Before I lose my mind."

Dancer lifted his head and said three words that reverberated around my skull for what felt like a lifetime. Making no sense, beyond my ability to either understand or comprehend.

"She's your daughter."

Things Get Freaky

"What are you talking about?" Numb, I turned from Dancer to, what had she called herself, Amber? They both looked serious. Her beautiful, Dancer like utter death. We didn't have long, but at this point in time I didn't care. I had to know.

"She's your daughter, Spark. She came to me, decided she wanted to meet you. But you were still denying magic and pretty low, and once I'd told her all about you, what was going on, she decided to wait. I'm sorry, but she made me promise and I said I'd let her know when you were back being yourself. Guess I left it a little late."

"This makes no sense. Amber, you look just like Sarah, so similar it's hard not to think of you as her, but whatever you think, I'm not your father. I don't even see how she's your mother. How old are you?"

"Forty-two."

"Oh." I studied her and as I looked, really looked for the first time, it was obvious it wasn't Sarah. The cheekbones were higher, the mouth smaller, nose more pointed and her frame more petite. It was all so long ago, it was incredible I remembered her well at all. She had features that could have been inherited from me. My blue, intense eyes, the slightly large forehead, the set of the jaw, but that could just as easily have been me looking for similarities and finding them, not meaning it was true. Hell, it couldn't be true.

"Look, um, Faz, can I call you Faz?"

"Sure, for now." Nobody called me Faz, just Kate and Grandma, but I was muddled and what if? No, it couldn't be. "Look, Sarah died forty-two years ago, you can't be her child. Can't be mine. She died, and I think I'd know if she gave birth."

Amber leaned forward and put her angelic head in her hands, eyes focused on mine. Then she glanced at Dancer for a moment and I saw him nod. "Okay, here goes." She sighed deeply, reached out for the ashtray beside her and lit the joint, inhaled sharply then set it back down. "This is all what I've pieced together after the fact, but I think it's close enough to the truth for it to be the explanation."

"Go on."

"Do you remember maybe a month or maybe two before Mum died? When you, er, had a final intimate encounter when she was feeling a little better?"

"I do," I said warily, memories flooding back, almost overwhelming me with grief. "She was between treatments, resting up, ready to go back into battle once she got her strength back. It didn't work, but anyway.

Yes, we had a final... Damn, what is wrong with me? Yes, we slept together a final time not long before she passed."

It broke my heart. That night we cried like we'd never cried before. Her body was a wreck. She hurt and ached and was bone weary. I asked if I should stop multiple times. No, she'd said, she needed this. The closeness, the connection, just in case it was the last time.

I'd joked, saying I'd ravage her silly once she got better, that I'd never let her out of bed even once she was back on her feet. We never slept together again.

"Faz? Faz?" Amber was calling my name but it was from far, far away. Like I was answering Sarah's call from the other side of the divide between life and death.

"Sorry, lots of memories. That night was special, more love wrapped up with us clinging to it, even though it hurt us both so much. Her more than me. But it was special, something different to how it had ever been before."

"So you felt it, then? That it was different? Special. Deeper and more intimate?" Amber watched me carefully, as if gauging my reaction and my words. Seeing if I confirmed something, although I didn't know what.

"It was an emotional time. She'd gone through so much, had so much more to go through. Ugh, can we change the subject please? This is getting depressing as hell and I'm already about as depressed as I can get."

"There was a note," said Amber. "Mum said that she did something that night, thinking it would be her final gift to you. That if she passed, if the treatments didn't work, then at least you would always have her gift."

"You?"

"Me," she said, nodding. "But then she was taken before she intended. She thought she'd at least see out the time to give birth."

"It surprised us all. She went downhill rapidly. It happened very quickly." Realization hit like a smack from a pissed-off troll to the guts. "You mean... she died thinking she'd lost her baby?"

"Yes."

"No, wait, this makes no sense. If she died then the fetus would have been only a few months old. And I would have known. Someone would have said."

"She made plans, Faz, right at the very end. I guess you knew she was a strong witch, that she was powerful?"

"Of course I did!" I said a little too testily. "Sorry, this is hard to take in. I don't understand. And, ugh." Deep nausea overwhelmed me as I lost myself again.

As I toppled sideways to the floor, I knew this was it. No waking as Faz Pound, Dark Magic Enforcer. I'd awake as zombie, nothing more, nothing less. Even if I kept my sense of self I'd still rip through Amber, my daughter—which was impossible—like she was nothing but meat. Nourishment for my corrupted soul.

Then all was blank. Black. Nothingness. And part of me welcomed it. No life, no pain. No more hurt.

The Cure

This time I awoke to find I was back in the living room, sitting on a rug and propped up against the sofa. Amber finished manhandling Dancer into position just as I opened my eyes.

She jumped back, eyes wide.

"Don't worry, I won't eat you. It's me, Faz."

"Oh, good. Damn, you guys gave me a scare."

"Sorry. Look, I don't know what to think about all this, but whatever the truth is I want you to know it's been lovely meeting you. I apologize if I said anything untoward. This is all messed up in my head. I don't know what's real and what's the infection. For all I know I'm not even here."

"It's okay, I understand."

Dancer moaned and we turned to him. He was close to the end now, and I was, too. His face was almost black, his breathing shallow, and he twitched like he was having a seizure. Tremors racked my body and I knew I'd been doing the same and looked just as bad.

"You want me to save you both? Get rid of the virus?"

"Oh, God, yes. You can do that?"

"Sure I can. That's why Dancer brought you here, right?"

"I guess. And to meet you."

"Haha, I may have only met him once before tonight but I get the feeling he's a good guy deep down. Not at all what he appears to be."

"Yeah, you're right. Although, if we get out of this alive, I am gonna kill him."

"Haha, he said you were funny."

"He did?"

"Yup. Right, let's get started. You first, or him?"

"Do Spark first," whispered Dancer, eyes opening slowly, his hand going to his hair automatically.

"No, you first, Dancer. You're worse than I am."

"Have you seen yourself? You look gross. Brains. BRAINS!"

"Brains! Ugh, whoever you do, please do it quick."

"Okay, okay, both at once. This will hurt and it will definitely freak you guys out, but you ready?" Amber finished her joint while we talked and the sweet smell hit my nostrils for a moment before it was buried under the scent of her, the scent of her flesh.

But there was something else apart from the craving for brains and human meat. Her scent was so familiar. This was Sarah's child, I knew it deep down on a primeval level. Every ounce of my being knowing it was true. Her scent was that of her mother's, and I no longer doubted.

"We're ready."

"Whatever you're gonna do, please do it now," I said, feeling urges begin to overwhelm me. My heart kept skipping beats and my pulse was weak and slow, the cravings morphing into a need almost impossible to resist.

"Okay, but you won't like it."

She wasn't lying.

It Begins

Amber stared us both down—she was an expert, even stoned—as if weighing our mettle, summing us up in a single, way too protracted gaze that left me feeling exposed. She nodded, seemingly satisfied, then turned from us and brought her long-suffering joint to life. She toked on what was little more than a butt until the doobie—that's still cool, right?—flared to life, then exhaled a heady cloud of smoke that veiled her.

I felt dizzy, the worst kind of light-headed, and shook my head to gain clarity as the inner zombie clawed at the gaps in my consciousness. I'd been opened up with a rusty can-opener and part of me scooped out, there's no other way to describe the feeling.

Dancer moaned beside me but I didn't have the energy to focus on him, to be concerned with my friend. No, all I could do was try to save myself as an uncaring numbness gripped my mind like spectral hands were crushing my brain between immensely strong fingers, squishy goop falling to the floor in wasted lumps that mocked my pathetic excuse of a life.

Sarah was still hazy, the smoke increasing in the room until I began to panic that we'd somehow been caught in a fire and would burn alive. Would I still be zombie if I went out like that? Damn, what was wrong with me? Of course I would.

I tried to stand, to call out, warn them, but my legs didn't work and my hands and arms were entirely ineffective. Accepting, I slumped back, all energy and will gone. It was just me, locked inside my own head, watching with only mild interest as the zombie stepped out of the shadows, ready to embrace me. To turn me at last.

But something changed, and as the smoke drifted lazily by I understood this was nothing but the incense and the cigarette Amber now puffed on between mumbling incoherent words in a deep voice that reminded me of those Tibetan monks that chanted high on their windswept mountain tops.

Amber's spell grew more intense and her call louder as the smoke eddied in increasingly violent patterns. Forces congregated in the room. Drawn by her call, her summoning.

Who was she? What was she? Was she really my child? How could that be? Such questions would have to wait. Already, the thoughts were drifting away, sucked out of me along with my desire to understand this woman, my need for answers. There was something stronger taking the place of my questions, it was a tugging at my very essence, at who I was and what I was. At the heart of the man, at what made me more than just a bloke called Faz. At what made me Black Spark.

She was sucking the magic right out of me!

I panicked. Deep, utter, mind-bendingly freaky-as-hell panic that stabbed at the core of the person I knew I was. The magic I'd finally come to accept made me whole. What defined me as a person, as a wizard. The truth that I was Hidden, immortal of sorts. A user and abuser of magic I no longer quite stole from the Empty but was granted permission to use when asked, all of that was being taken from me.

Amber was like me!

My daughter was sucking not only on her cigarette, but between lungfuls of nicotine she was imbibing the nature of what I had become, what I'd accepted.

Amber was taking my magic and she was powerful. She could do it and there was nothing I could do to stop it in my weakened state. Hell, I wasn't sure I'd be able to stop her even if I was in top condition.

I felt her strength, her power, her abilities as she breathed me in. My mouth was forced open and my head snapped back with a loud crack. As I struggled to hold on to my sense of self, my throat expanded and magic from my core forced its way out my mouth.

My tattoos flared briefly then flatlined. All power gone. I tried to call to the Empty, to ask for just a little help to save me from this deranged daughter of mine, but the call wasn't answered. She had control, was blocking my attempts, and the most annoying thing was she did it exactly how I did it to others. This was my specialty. Nobody else had this skill—it was what made me so called upon by those having trouble with magic miscreants.

She was better.

I would be empty, would be lost and back to being just a man. No chance of ever becoming what I once was. The ways of magic would be blocked, a barrier put in place to stop me ever brimming over with magic again. My ink would never channel powerful forces, direct the magic until it did my bidding. I would never be able to call on it in my time of need, protect myself from the supernatural beasties that would come for me now I was a Regular.

True, complete panic set in as I experienced for the first time what it was I'd done to countless others. My one true companion over the endless years, who I'd shunned and cursed and cried over and reveled in and screamed with joy at the power she gave, she would be gone and I'd never get her back.

I tried to scream as I felt a deep ball of magic solidify deep inside the pit of my stomach, to rage at her and tell her no. That she had said she would help but was destroying me. If she was my daughter then why was she doing this?

But screams didn't emerge from my taut throat. No, a fat lump of ephemeral magic tore through my system and scratched up my esophagus. As my hands went to my neck—sure it was nothing but jagged flesh but finding it smooth and slick with sweat—my jaw hinged wide and pellets of magic spat from my mouth. Black as my anger and strong as my hatred for what she was doing.

They shot across the gap between us and blew holes in the screen of smoke that shrouded her, and I watched, aghast, as the smoke cleared to reveal the essence of what I was being sucked on down. Other lumps of magic were coming to her, and I turned my head enough to see that Dancer, who I'd forgotten entirely, was being treated in a similar fashion.

Again, and again, magic was ripped from our systems, our chakras stripped bare, our bodies sucked dry. Taking drags of her cigarette between the more dangerous and volatile breaths containing all we'd worked to achieve.

All the toil and trouble, the strife and bliss, it was being consumed casually by this woman as if it were nothing.

She wafted a languid hand and the gathering smoke parted around her face again. Her eyelids were heavy, her face a mask of focus and determination, and she winked at me as she breathed deep. Then her happiness vanished and she hunched forward, screaming in utter agony as our magic hit her system.

Amber's face darkened, black veins appearing on her face like a spider's web had been slapped onto her skin, and her features morphed into those of the undead.

Her eyes rolled up in her head and for a moment all that could be seen was a milky white. Then she screamed again and globs of tainted magic shot from her mouth in a streamer of corruption, gushing up into the air and merging with the smoke before fading like a dream through the ceiling.

She lowered her head, wiped at her brow, and smiled a smile that somehow felt comforting. The smile of my daughter. The smile of family.

"Right, let's get started," she said.

Oh shit. I though that was it, but it was only the beginning.

An Interruption

As Amber spoke I gained a sudden clarity. And I have to admit I was mightily impressed. Not only did she have abilities akin to mine, she could go beyond what I'd accomplished. Amber had enough skill to take specifics of magic from whomsoever she wished. Unsurprisingly, there was a cost.

When I suck the magic right out of Hidden, I take on their power along with something more personal. I almost become them, their essence soaked up like a sponge along with their magic. I spit that tainted essence right back out as soon as I can, along with the magic they have accumulated, but I can't pick and choose what I take. I draw their whole magic, all of it, out of them.

It seemed Amber could be more choosy with her efforts. She had the skill to remove sections of it, to leave you with your abilities even as she removed the corrupted parts, the parts she wanted to take. She could stop you being able to channel it in certain ways, stop you being able to control it for certain acts if she so desired, or, in our case, remove infected, corrupt magic that was the cause of the zombie infection.

What she'd done so far was nothing more than a taste of what was to come. She'd located the virus, had removed what I guess you could call an outer coating. The husk of protection within which the virus had been wrapped up safe and sound, seeping into us like a slow release capsule, one of those squishy tablets with liquid inside. She had left the virus exposed and weakened, drifting in our systems without the control and direction it had before.

Boy did it hurt.

This wasn't the end, though, this wasn't even a true beginning. A magical aperitif, the main course yet to come.

"You guys taste gross," Amber said, giving us another sweet smile, her face framed by her shining hair. Almost white through the haze of incense and yet another cigarette.

"And you're an angel," said Dancer, his understanding of what was happening catching up with mine.

"You okay?" I asked, words feeling alien in my mouth, my tongue still swollen and my throat raw from the expunging of the zombie husk.

"Yeah, just about." Amber drew deep on her cigarette and again my vision clouded as she disappeared behind her screen of smoke.

I watched the patterns swirl and eddy, everything sucked in through her mouth as she breathed in deep and her chest expanded. Like the center of a whirlpool, everything drawn into the depths of a truly powerful witch. If that's what she was. To be honest, I was at a loss how to classify her. She didn't give off a vibe like she was a witch, seemed fairly neutral, but I'd met such Hidden before, and usually it meant they were a lot more powerful than I could comprehend so I wasn't looking in the right place.

My head snapped up, my back arched, and what felt like a thousand volts fired into my brain then shot through my tattoos. I was left gasping, sweating, and wondering if my ink had burst in a million places.

The process began in earnest.

It was different this time, more intense and yet more liberating. She was removing the infection piece by tainted piece. I felt the heat and the tight swelling of my leg recede, felt my whole body suddenly relax as I slumped forward when the virus was drawn away from my system and down into the place it all began, curling up tight at the source of the bite.

This was the perpetual death zombies endured. An immortality of the most corrupt kind that gave life beyond death and allowed the infected to keep on moving when it shouldn't be possible to do so. This was the part that reanimated the carrier.

Weaker and weaker it became, the magic that had insinuated itself throughout my body reversing progress and regrouping at the source. My limbs were my own once more, my mind too, back to being a man not a monster. My true Hidden self restored. I felt the change within, felt my cells, my blood, my heart, my mind, all of it be released from the stranglehold.

The part of the virus that gave life after death was condensed into a tight ball at my leg. The magic I had accumulated and that which was now an inherent part of me restored to all its pure and wondrous glory.

I reached down, entranced by the act, and still utterly under Amber's thrall I felt a lump grow at my thigh. I spread my fingers apart and fought to remain calm as a fiery red bulge grew and grew like a tumor. The skin spread tight then tighter still, then as thin as paper. I screamed and howled and heard Dancer do likewise. Amber yelled then the world spun on its axis.

The skin split and a foul, blasphemous lump of dark, ghostly meat tore at the skin as if it were emerging from an egg.

The poisonous ball of venom hurtled through the smoke, spreading and becoming little more than a darker patch of air. It collided with a similar presence that I could only assume emanated from Dancer, and the collision further distributed the already broken power.

The smoke cleared as it slammed into Amber's mouth, forcing her back a few feet. She was wild, hair blowing like she was in a cheap shampoo commercial, her features contorted with effort as she struggled with the essence of the undead she'd taken upon herself.

She froze, body rigid, and I wondered if she'd gone too far. That she'd taken on our pain and suffering only to drop down dead.

Then she shook, great spasms that sent her arms flailing and her head snapping left then right. I knew, just knew, that she had died for a moment, as Dancer and I had done, but it passed in less than a second and she had control.

She coughed, not just any old cough, but a gut-wrenching purge of all the foulness she'd consumed, and out it came, worse than the preliminary ingestion of our infection by orders of magnitude.

Terrible, foul and malodorous lumps of magical disease erupted from her stretched mouth and shot upward, slammed into the ceiling in fat lumps, spread out across the entire room then slowly faded away. Cleansed and cured of all nastiness as the magic returned to the Empty.

Amber lowered her head and the first thing she did was light up a cigarette.

"Right, now it's time to get rid of the cravings. That's the reanimated part dealt with, no more chance of you guys being true zombie. We just have to deal with the other issue now."

"Oh, wow! I feel so much better," said Dancer waving his arm about, showing no concern for the gaping hole in his forearm, the ragged tatters of flesh and the exposed bone.

"Me too. That was amazing," I said, staring in wonder at the mess of split flesh that was my thigh.

Even as we spoke, our magic was busy repairing the damage. Flesh was knitting back together, veins and torn muscle strands fixing themselves at incredible speed as if our bodies rejoiced in the chance to function properly after so long without such control.

"It's not over," warned Amber. "You won't turn into zombies if you die, and the infection that kills you is gone, but you aren't out of the woods yet. Hold still, the next part is the most crucial. If I don't get it perfect, take exactly the right thing, you'll be lost to yourselves. I have to remove the hunger, the obsession with what sustains the zombie. It's much more elusive, and a lot harder to find, so whatever you do don't move and don't resist."

Amber stared at her cigarette butt curiously, as if surprised she'd finished it, then stubbed it out in an ashtray.

"We have a lot of things to talk about once this is over," I said, wondering where we could start, still unable to comprehend how she was even alive if her mother had died when she was a two-month-old bean in her womb.

"We do," said Amber, holding my gaze. "Okay, time to get this over with."

Amber breathed deep and spread her arms wide in what can only be described as purely for the drama. This is it, I thought, she's actually doing it.

There was an almighty crash from the hall, sounding like a mirror breaking, and two very large and very goony goons stormed into the living room.

Ignoring us completely, hardly even glancing our way, one picked Amber up under his arm, and before we had time to react, so out of it were we, they were gone, simply vanished.

"Fucking vampires," I moaned, which I thought was rather apt given the circumstances.

Feeling Kinda Funny

I scrambled to my feet, body feeling strange because I was in complete control once again. I'd forgotten what it was like to have total dominance over my own limbs and I felt light, almost like air. Everything worked as it should, moved where I wanted it to, did what I wanted. And what I wanted right now was to tear Dancer's flesh from his body, rip it into long strips of meaty morsels and let the slimy goodness slide down my throat.

Smash. I wanted to smash him real good. Grab his head in my hands swollen with magic and yank. Spin it around and around until it twisted off. Suck it. Suck out his brains like ice cream from the bottom of a chewed-off cornet and let the gray goodness satiate my overwhelming hunger.

"Um, I think we need to find her, and fast," I said, words garbled as I stared Dancer in the eyes, my hands tight around his throat, his gripping me just as firmly.

"That's a very good idea."

"On three?" Dancer nodded. "One, two, three. Release." We let go at the same time and took a quick step back from each other.

"Spark, I really, really want to eat your brains right now. Brains!" Dancer recoiled in horror and the worst thing of it all was I wasn't shocked.

It seemed like a perfectly normal thing to say, mainly because I felt exactly the same. Oh, he smelled so tasty, and that was gross, or it should have been. He always smelled of death, of formaldehyde and damp soil, of the places the dead are laid to rest. Or often not.

He smelled yummy. Of brains and goopy bits, and warm flesh.

"I want to eat you, too. We have to fight this, dude. If we don't, it's gonna be one helluva tea party."

"What happened? Who were those guys?" asked Dancer, like I had the answers.

"You tell me," I said, shrugging. I didn't feel as concerned as I should have, the overriding urge to tear flesh forcing everything else to fade into the background like an afterthought.

"How would I know?" Dancer gripped his hands tight, knuckles white, just to stop himself lunging for me.

"Because she came to you and told you who she was. You must know things about her. Don't tell me you didn't investigate her because I know for a fact you would have. You don't let people like that into our lives without going over them with a fine-tooth comb."

"Okay, I may have done a little digging, but I didn't come up with all the goods. She's a bit of a mystery woman in case you haven't noticed."

"Aaw, hell, what is wrong with us? We gotta go get her. If she is my daughter and—"

"She is."

I gave him the daggers for interrupting. "If she is, then I want to know how, and if not, well, we still have to save her. Come on, let's go. You can tell me what you know on the way."

"The way where?"

Damn, but he had a good point. The vamps would be long gone. I had no idea where they could have taken her, or how to track her in a hurry. "Guess we need to go back to the car."

"Spark, you know that's a very bad idea, right?"

"Yeah, tell me about it."

Yummy

Closing the door on the suburban dream felt otherworldly. It was as if nothing had happened. From the outside, the house looked quiet and exactly like every other one in the street. Amazing what goes on behind closed doors, right?

We checked the road, looking fruitlessly for a sign of where they might have gone. As expected, there was nothing. No hint or clue to help us start our search.

Part of me, okay, most of me, didn't even care. Emotions were crippled, stunted little nubs of things that took a backseat to the important stuff—feeding my soul with the essence of others. Taking their hopes and dreams, their power and their life force and stuffing it inside until I was fit to burst.

I knew I'd been right about the virus, that the root of the problem was a need to feed off the truth of what it was to be human. The rest was just background noise to allow the feeding to continue indefinitely. Being dead yet not dead gave the zombie the ability to continually top up on this primordial energy that permeated the universe. It allowed them to focus like no human had ever focused before. To be single-minded and utterly driven.

Hardly ideal when you just discovered you had a daughter, and now you'd met her she was taken, and was the only person who could make you whole again. Talk about lazy parenting—I'd win awards if it wasn't for the fact I couldn't be arsed to show up and collect.

"Come on, let's go," said Dancer cautiously, keeping an eye on me.

"Fine, but don't try anything funny," I warned.

We split up, walking either side of the center line of the road, checking each other constantly as we walked. "Tell me what you know. All of it."

"I will, but first I want to say sorry, again."

"You've said that too many times already. How could you do this to me? How could you keep it from me?"

"Because you were being a moody bugger and it was her choice. We're friends, but that doesn't mean I disregard other people's feelings entirely. She was confused, a little scared, and unsure of what she wanted. She said she wanted to meet you, or thought maybe she did, but needed to be sure the timing was right."

"So, what happened?"

"You. You happened. You were fighting your demons, deciding if you wanted to be involved in our world or not. I told her what you'd been through, about your decision, and she thought it best to wait."

"That all makes sense. But what doesn't is you not telling me she was out here somewhere or even that she existed."

Dancer stopped and stepped away from me, the cravings clearly intensifying. "What would have been the point? Tell you that you have a daughter but she's steering clear until you sort your head out? Like that would have made you come to your decision any sooner. It would have just clouded your judgment."

I thought for a while, pushing down the intense need to poke out his eyes with my fingers and lick the juices from the seeping sockets. "Damn, I hate it when you're right."

"Haha, that's why I'm Head. I know this is tough, I can't imagine how tough, but it was best to wait. If all this mess hadn't happened then I would have got in touch with her and we could have set things up properly. But she warned me, Spark. She told me that under no circumstances was I to tell you about her or try to push things. If I did then she'd be gone, would know, and that would be it."

"So what's she afraid of?"

Dancer looked at me like I'd lost what little sense I had. "Isn't it obvious? She got caught up in something and wanted it to be on her own terms. My guess is she didn't want anyone to know about you since it could put you in danger as you'd obviously try to protect her from whatever is happening."

"And why would she think that if she didn't know me?"

"Brains. Lovely brains. Mmm." Dancer's body shook and he got a faraway look in his eyes as he recovered and began walking toward me.

"Dancer, careful, buddy." He lunged for me. I slapped away his arm and shouted right in his ear, "DANCER!" He jumped back, freaked, and grabbed his own arm as it reached out for me again.

"Hell, we have to get this sorted."

"True. The only thing worse than being a zombie is being alive and still wanting human bits and bobs."

"Ugh, this is so nasty. I feel gross." He shook like a dog and then continued. "You don't know quite what a reputation you have, do you?"

"How'd you mean?" I asked, nonplussed.

"Black Spark, Dark Magic Enforcer, is pretty damn popular. Everyone in our world knows who you are. I mean everyone. The handsome guy with the bleached hair who traveled to Japan to avenge his family, killed the most powerful female vampire in the world. You're legend. There are even comics about you."

"Haha, very funny. I just did what I had to do. No reason anyone else would be interested." Why would they? It was personal.

"But you still did it. You went under the skinner's knife and emerged triumphant. I don't even want to think about how famous you'll be once word spreads about Dragon and the damn dwarves."

"I guess, but it's just work. And it's not like I actually defeated him, anyway. Lots of my jobs don't work out how I planned them, you know that."

"Sure I do, and I also know that you're one lucky bugger. That's part of the mystique, though. The wizard who always triumphs. It doesn't matter how, your jobs always work out in the end. Young trainees worship you. Why do you think Mithnite is so damn happy to be taken under your wing?"

"Cause he was homeless?"

"You are such a dick at times," said Dancer.

"Hey! That's my line, and you're the dick." I thought for a moment then asked, "Do you really think I'm handsome?"

"As I said. Dick."

I'd never thought of myself as having much of a reputation. Not outside Cardiff, anyway. Sure, I was one of the best in the city, but it's a small place. And yes, I got called on for jobs from other places, from other Hidden now and then, but I'd usually been tied up working for Rikka, so often turned them down. And since Japan? I'd stayed off-grid, refused all offers of work and kept my head down. Not thinking my exploits with Kimiko would be of any interest to those outside my immediate circle. Guess I was wrong.

"Hey, where can I get the comics? Do I look good?"

"No, you don't. They gave you too many muscles and not enough pain-in-the-assness. And most of it is wildly exaggerated."

"Oh, sounds great," I said, feeling somewhat cheery for the first time since the nibble incident.

We continued walking away from suburbia and back to the car. I had so many questions I didn't know where to begin. So I started at the beginning. "Do you think she really is my daughter? How is it possible? That story about Sarah being pregnant and then dying with the fetus only two months old, that can't be true. Can it?"

"Honestly? I don't know how she's your daughter, what happened after Sarah died to make this possible. But this is the Hidden world we're talking about, so you know anything can happen."

"No, it can't. Things like this absolutely do not happen. C'mon."

"Fine, it's a new one on me. But let me ask you a question. Is she your daughter?"

"Yes," I said, knowing it was true. "She is. I don't know how, or what the truth is behind her story, but she's mine and Sarah's, I'm sure of it."

"There you go, then. The minute I saw her I knew she was yours. She looks like you, but also has your aura, something of you inside her. Shame about the hippie thing, but then nobody has perfect kids."

"This is crazy. She's older than Kate. I can't have a daughter older than my girlfriend."

"Not a lot you can do about it, is there? Oh, we're here."

We stopped at the entrance to the alley, and as we peered around the corner to make sure that nothing had happened while we were gone, I caught a scent so beautiful, so intoxicating and overpowering I lost my mind.

Dancer growled beside me, a deep, ancient rumble of the hunter fixated on his prey.

We stepped out into the alley's entrance and with tattered rags for clothes, stinking of old blood and fresh marijuana, incense and cigarette smoke, we sprinted down the alley, arms clawing wildly, utterly lost to ourselves.

The rest is a total blur. I was so deep into dreams of flesh it was maddening. I would rip these tasty treats to shreds and no way would I share.

Lady Trouble

"Do not move," warned Persimmon.

I didn't.

"What happened?" I asked, then panicked a little. "Um, does talking count as moving? Cause if it does then I'll be quiet."

"Dick," muttered Persimmon before getting off my chest where she'd been sitting, knife at my throat, leaving me under no doubt she'd use it if she had to.

I could have blasted her, I was sure, as Faz Pound was back feeling rather fine, at least right now, but you don't do that to friends, even if they are doing the whole sharp blade at throat thing.

Persimmon got to her feet with a single bounce, and I sat up with only a slight, manly groan. Okay, I whined and said, "No fair," but I felt manly.

As I used the wall for balance to help me stand, I took in the scene and noted that Mithnite was backed up across the alley, an aura of magic surrounding him for protection, his eyes focused and his hands ready to do the nasty on yours truly.

"Where's Dancer?" I asked. "And Kate, is she okay?"

"I'm down here," came a voice from the other side of the car.

"And I'm about a millimeter from his neck," came the beautiful tones of my vampire girlfriend.

"Hope you two aren't cheating on me. That's pretty low, guys." I gave an apologetic smile and raised my eyebrows to show I was sorry for whatever I'd done, knowing it wouldn't have been anything friendly, and wandered around to where they were.

Dancer got up, Kate right next to him, and remained very, very still. One look at Kate made it obvious why. Her teeth were bared, milky vampire venom dripping onto his ruined shirt. Dancer was trying to smile to placate Kate but it made him look like he was attempting a bad vampire impression.

"You two okay?" I asked, "Not done anything too bad have we?"

"Don't get clever, Faz. Now isn't the time for jokes," warned Kate as she released her grip from his throat and he dropped the few inches to the ground.

"Sorry. What happened?"

"I think you need to tell us that, don't you?" Kate's teeth receded and she stepped away from Dancer, and me—boy did that make me feel all kinds of awful.

"Hell, I honestly don't know where to begin."

Persimmon came up from behind and said, "Why not start with you two guys not looking like the bloody walking dead anymore but charging down the alley screaming "Brains, brains," and almost munching on poor Mithnite here. Poor kid almost got his brains sucked out his ears."

"I'm not a kid," Mithnite protested, staying close to the wall.

"Oh, shit. Sorry, dude. Look, we, er, went to see Dancer's contact and she got rid of the virus, at least the part that makes you turn, but we, er, got interrupted before she could take away the cravings."

"That's awful," said Kate, "But good, too, right?"

"Kind of," said Dancer, trying to smooth down his clothes and look respectable. It was utterly pointless. He was as much of a state as me—we needed a tailor, and fast. Did they do all night suit making these days? I guessed not, especially around here.

"No, it is. We won't turn, and I can't tell you how much better I feel. Actually, I feel goddamn awesome. Full of magic and power. Like I could just float up in the air I'm so connected to the Empty. Getting rid of the virus's effects on the body has brought me back to myself at full capacity and then some. Um, er... What the hell?"

My view was skewed, as if everyone were crouching down and I was growing taller at the same time. Then I realized what was happening and why everyone was looking at me so weirdly. It wasn't because of my monologue, it was because I was floating.

"You're levitating," said an awed Mithnite. "That is so cool. Will you teach me? How'd you do it?"

"I dunno. I was feeling good and—Argh." The moment I thought about it, I crashed to the dirty alley in a heap like the ground had been taken out from under me.

"Faz! What is happening? You've never done that before. That's not how you normally use magic."

I took Kate's offered hand, the fact we'd attacked them seemingly forgotten, and she hauled me to my feet with ease. "I don't know how I did it. Guess I'm becoming the new, improved me now I've got my magic back. Damn, we need to go find Amber and get this finished with."

"Amber? Who's Amber?" asked Kate, giving me the evil eye and then switching to suspicious—she's got both looks down to a T.

"Er, my daughter."

I didn't even have time to flinch, let alone duck, before Kate smacked me square in the face and I was thrown across the alley hitting the slimy brick wall with one helluva thud.

An Explanation

I may have managed an "Urgle," or maybe just an "Ugh," then decided to remain sitting in the puddle leaning against the wall I'd been rather unjustly slammed into on account of something I had no control over and had a hard time believing.

"You better talk, buddy, and fast," ordered Kate as she loomed over me looking about as angry as I'd ever seen her. And I once ate her cheat day muffin, so you can be sure I'd seen her at her most ferocious.

"Can I get out of the puddle? Can I have a kiss?"

"No you may not!" Kate actually stamped her foot, and she splashed me. It was one of those days. Nights. Whatever. Lifetimes, probably.

I noted with some concern that everyone else was standing well away from us, right when I needed the support.

"Traitors," I said, then held up my hands to protect me from my beautiful lady's wrath. "Kate, this isn't my fault. This woman, Amber, and she's very pretty by the way. Although, you know, not as pretty as you. Obviously." I wasn't winning her over, which was odd, so I tried harder.

"It's Dancer's fault. He knew all about it. He knew and didn't tell." Okay, look, you weren't there. She was ready to rip my head off. And don't forget about the puddle.

"Why you slimy son-of-a—"

"Sorry, dude, all's fair in love and lady vampire wrath."

Kate's head whipped around to lay that wrath on Dancer, but he'd decided now was the perfect time to try to eat Persimmon. He got that distant look in his eyes and licked his thin lips then snapped at her like a rabid dog, lost to himself.

Good job we'd forgotten we were powerful Hidden when this craving struck, as otherwise I don't doubt that all three of them would have been dead by now. As it was, Persimmon just backhanded him across the cheek and his head snapped to the side as she knocked the hunger right out of him.

"Ow!"

"What is with you guys?" said Persimmon, not knowing whether to step toward me or Dancer or just run the hell away. I would have run.

"Sorry, we're a little messed up. It's been a weird time of it lately."

"Enough," screamed Kate. "Will someone please tell me what you are talking about. And will you please stop trying to eat us. It's getting really annoying."

I got up while nobody was looking and kept my back to the wall. "Okay, here's the deal," I said, "but no more hitting. It's kind of demeaning and we aren't in the best of condition."

"Just spill it, mister, before I knock you right into next week. And trust me, I'll be there waiting for you, with a damn big stick to whack you with."

I spilled it.

*

"Well, am I off the hook?" I asked nervously, wondering why everyone was so quiet. I raised my eyes from the ground and understood why nobody was speaking. "What are you all crying for?"

"That's so sad," said Mithnite.

"You poor thing," said Persimmon.

"You went through all that? That explains why you hate hospitals," said Kate.

"Everyone hates hospitals," muttered Dancer, the only one not weeping.

"Dick," said Persimmon.

"I don't hate hospitals," I protested.

"Faz, you big fat liar. You made me go in on my own that time I visited Penelope. Said they made you too depressed."

"Yeah, well, they are depressing. Anyway, I'm forgiven?"

"Of course! I can't imagine what that must have been like, watching someone you love die. You never said." Kate took my hand, a big risk considering I could get the hunger at any moment.

"It was a long time ago. Everything fades, even that."

"But you have a daughter! Are you sure? It sounds crazy."

"Kate, I know, I didn't believe it, either. It's not possible but at the same time she is mine, I can feel it. You will, too, when you meet her."

"And she's older than me. Not sure I like that." Kate smiled, trying to lighten the mood, but it wasn't easy.

Everyone felt it, the all-pervading sense of things spiraling out of control all over again. Out of the frying pan, into the raging inferno that was our Hidden life.

"Damn, if I'd known you guys got up to so much mental stuff I'd have asked to live with you years ago," said Mithnite, looking way too eager and pleased now he'd wiped away the tears. "Naked boobies, dragons, gold, zombies, ancient wizards, exploding stuff all over the place. Lost daughters, and heart-rending stories, this stuff rocks." We all stared at him, astonished. "You know, it's sad and all and awful, but c'mon, you guys get up to some crazy stuff."

"Were you staring at my boobs?" asked Persimmon, stepping toward Mithnite.

The poor lad turned beetroot and inadvertently glanced down at Persimmon's now concealed chest. "Um, no. Ugh, sorry, couldn't help it. Help, guys?"

"No chance, you're on your own, mate. I know better than to look at naked ladies unless specifically asked to," I said, feeling pleased with such a genuine reply.

"Liar," accused Kate.

With the ice broken and mood lightened, and heartfelt thanks going out to Mithnite and Persimmon for doing it, I think we realized simultaneously that we needed to get our act together fast if we were to finish this all off without either me or Dancer having to be dealt with in a rather more serious and deadly fashion.

"Okay," said Kate, "show me the house. Let me get a sniff of her and we'll track her down."

"Hey, if anyone's going to do the tracking it will be me," said Persimmon. "I'm the shifter here."

"And I'm the vampire. I can track the vampires if I get a hint of them. So I guess you guys lucked out. You have the perfect predators on your side."

"Perfect in every way," said Dancer, smiling at Persimmon.

"You okay? Do you need the loo?"

"What? No, I was smiling."

"Oh, sorry, thought maybe you'd overdone the fiber."

"Let's go," I said, terrible urges surfacing once again. "Brains!"

I lunged, and I got smacked down again. It was becoming a major inconvenience.

On the Hunt

Watching women with their noses in the air, nostrils flaring, as they take in the scent of prey is oddly mesmerizing. Maybe it's the way the chest expands, or the way they are so focused, or maybe it's the sparkle in the eyes as certain molecular combinations hit and they cock their head to the side and grin, knowing they've found something.

Or, and I suspect this is more likely, it's just me and I have issues.

Either way, Kate and Persimmon had a fix on not only Amber, but the vampires, too.

"Should we walk or take the car?" I asked as we retreated from Amber's front door.

"Car," they both chimed, looking at me like I was dumb.

"What, do I have something in my hair?" I asked, putting a hand to the mop just as much in need of a wash as the rest of me.

"No, you just look like an utter perv," said Kate. "And stop licking your lips, it's weird."

I kept quiet. Damn, and there I was thinking I was being circumspect about my nostril fetish. Yeah, another one to add to the list.

We piled into the car and Kate drove slowly with the windows down. Us guys remained silent while Kate and Persimmon discussed which way they believed the trail led, sometimes stopping, sometimes speeding up on long stretches of road. All the while, they repeatedly stuck their heads out the window trying to keep track of the elusive scent.

Soon we were out of the town and enveloped in darkness. Unfamiliar darkness.

It's odd, but being in the countryside at home feels safe. Familiar and comforting. But being in the dark, surrounded by tall hedges and looming oaks when in unknown territory made me feel anything but happy.

Why? Because there are things. Always things. And these things didn't know me here. Might not be as responsive to the fact Dancer was Head of the UK Hidden Council and their boss, the guy in charge. Or, they might know full well who we all were, and that might make it worse, not better.

As Kate and Persimmon remained focused on the hunt and we switched back this way and that in the maze of lanes until nobody knew where we were or what direction we were headed, I let their voices, and Mithnite's constant stream of questions fielded expertly by Dancer—which mostly consisted of him saying either, "Dunno," or, "Shut up," or plain ignoring him—fade and tried to think things through.

It was hard, as the hunger kept creeping up on me and if it wasn't for some magic focus now I was in control again, I would have been gnawing on Mithnite's arm in a heartbeat.

As it was, both Dancer and I had this under control, for a while, but I didn't hold out much hope long term unless we found Amber and got her to use her special skills.

And that was just one of many mysteries. How did she do it? She'd be about as sought after as you can get if the Hidden world knew of her abilities, as not only would it make her a damn good enforcer if she had the other skills for the job—namely putting up with being hit and attacked on a regular basis—but she would be in demand from many other Hidden.

No end of people in our world find themselves with magic they'd rather do without. From ingesting potions that have adverse side-effects, to being hexed, to being possessed, to finding the magic they thought they could control was making them do weird stuff, or acquired skills that were anything but welcome. We mess up constantly, unable to control the forces from the Hidden that are stolen and less than suited to most no matter how adept they believe themselves to be.

Was that why she kept such a low profile all these years? I'd certainly never heard of her, or anyone speak of a witch that had such power, and neither had Dancer.

That meant the Hidden world at large had no idea she even existed, and that ain't easy.

Magic users can never stay in the Regular world. It just never works out. There's always somebody to recognize the skills you try to hide from human Hidden or a preternatural creature that sees right through whatever disguise you try to use.

No, she was a true enigma all right, and her Hidden side was just the start of this woman of mystery's story.

I racked my brain trying to come up with an explanation for what she'd told me. I accepted that she believed it to be true, and maybe it was. That her mother, my wife, had died when she was no larger than a pea, but then what?

How had she survived? How was that possible? I'd seen Sarah dead and cold. No child can survive after a mother passes away, not at that age.

I came to only one conclusion. It wasn't possible. Either Amber was lying or she'd been lied to.

Or... No, I'd know that, too. A supernatural creature, that emerged from the womb somehow transformed into a child that could cope with the world? It was ridiculous and couldn't happen, certainly not from two human parents, so there had to be another explanation.

Amber was sure to finish her story once we were cured, saved by her skill, so I leaned back against the seat, sighed, and decided not to think about it any more. I'd just wait until we found her and I could get answers direct.

As long as she wasn't killed by the goons or whoever they worked for, of course.

Enough!

"Stop the car," I screamed. "Right now."

Kate slammed on the brakes and everyone turned to me then glanced nervously out the window, but all anyone could see was the road ahead and the hedges lit up by the car's headlights.

"What's wrong? Can you see someone?" asked Dancer looking truly exhausted. Man, I knew how he felt.

"No, I can't see anyone. But I can't stand this a moment longer."

"What are you talking about?" asked Kate.

"I think he's lost his marbles," said Persimmon.

"You gonna get all bitey again?" asked Mithnite.

"Will everyone please be quiet. Hell, I can't hear myself think with everyone talking. Sorry." I knew I was being dramatic but it was true. I can't work under conditions like this. I need to be alone to figure things out, to follow up on things in the best way I see fit. Not have everyone talking and chiming in about how best to react to a situation nobody knew anything about.

So far there had been endless discussions about what the vamps wanted with Amber, who she was, what she was, what she may or may not have become involved in, and on and on it went. Speculation that made me increasingly tense until I was a ball of bunched nerves and about to scream.

Which is what I'd done, yes, I know.

I needed to deal with this in a more Black Spark manner. Meaning, I needed to be alone. It's how I work best, how things always work out, or usually, the last few days had been the antithesis of how I dealt with my jobs. I hadn't had enough time to myself, had gone from one insane situation to another. And if all that wasn't bad enough there was now a daughter in the mix and it was driving me nuts.

"Well, you could have just asked nicely," said Kate.

"Oh, shit, did I just say all that out loud?" I asked, my head so muddled I wasn't sure if I'd just been thinking those things or saying them.

"If you mean about us driving you nuts and you needing to be alone, and our ruminations on all this craziness that are making you bonkers, then yes, you said it out loud. You're one weird guy, Spark, you know that, right?" Persimmon looked at me funny, then gave Kate a sympathetic smile, like she was a saint for putting up with me. I guess she was.

"Sorry, sorry, but you guys know how I deal with things. I can't focus. My head's all over the place, and this is bloody serious, guys. Deadly."

"So what do you want to do?" asked Dancer, probably the one in the best position to know exactly how I operated and how I functioned best. After all, we went back a long way, and although I'd dealt with him a lot when he'd been Rikka's right-hand man, we never did many actual jobs together. He knew the score, in other words, and knew that to get the best from this enforcer he had to be left alone to figure it out solo.

"I want to know you're all safe. I want to know where Amber is. I want you all to get very far away while I go get her and deal with whatever she's involved in. And I really, really want her to cure me and Dancer of this damn hunger. I'm losing my mind here and don't know how long I can take it before I just explode and run around eating anything that's still got a pulse."

"Well," Dancer said cautiously, "that sounds like a plan to me. As Head, I hereby sanction Spark to save Amber and bring her back so she can also stop me eating anything with a brain. Preferably still warm," he added, then put a hand to his mouth in shock at the words he'd inadvertently spoken.

"You guys are definitely nuts," said Persimmon. "It's official."

"No more arguments. Find out where Amber is then leave," said Dancer. He didn't sound like the

Dancer we'd all come to love—or put up with—he sounded like the boss he was.

"I'm not going to do that. No way am—"

"Enough!" Dancer warned. "Kate, I know Spark well enough to know that if he's working solo he'll have a much better chance of doing this. What, you think we can all just barge in and grab Amber, wherever she may be?"

"Actually, yes. Because she's right over there." Kate pointed out the window into the darkness.

"Oh," I said, which sounded rather lame even to me, and I know lame.

A Recky

"You sure?" I asked.

"Yes. How about you, Persimmon, you sense it, too?" asked Kate.

"Definitely."

"Everyone wait here. I'm gonna go for a recky and —"

"What's a recky?" interrupted Mithnite.

"A reconnaissance, to check it out," I explained. "Damn, you really are still a total noob, aren't you?"

"That's what I'm here for," said Mithnite happily. I think he was having way too much fun with all this madness. Ah, the joys of youth.

"As I was saying. I'll go check it out then come back. If it's a vamp stronghold then there's no point trying to get Amber now, it's asking for trouble. Can you find somewhere quiet to pull in, Kate?"

"I don't like this," said Kate. "You should let me go. If it is vampires then it's better if they see me than you."

"But they won't see me, that's the point. Please?"

"Fine." Kate drove off slowly and within minutes we found a small lay-by with a signpost showing walkers the routes they could take around the surrounding countryside. Perfect.

I knew there would be more arguments, so before anyone could object further I jumped out the car and said, "Be back soon. Wait here and do not follow me. The last thing we need is for us all to get into trouble. Okay?"

There were grumbles and several very good reasons as to why this was a terrible idea, but I think my outburst of earlier and Dancer's agreement that I was better on my own had hit home. My reputation preceded me and they all knew I got the job done one way or another.

So, trying not to smile despite the severity of the situation, anticipating being alone now I had my sense back—at least a little—I stepped away from the car and was swallowed whole by the darkness of the British countryside.

There is something immensely satisfying about being alone in the dark, even though it's scary when you know for sure there are nasties lurking. You lose yourself, you test yourself, and you discover more about yourself than any doctor could ever tell you.

Darkness, true darkness, brings to the surface all your fears and insecurities. Your mind plays tricks on you, every sound amplified, and you become hyper-alert to danger and the unexpected. You have to battle these fears head on, to acknowledge them and then dismiss them or you'll be frozen. Or, worse. Lost and manic as you crash through the undergrowth in a desperate attempt to get away from the scariest thing in this world. Your own mind.

I was old enough and wise enough to know this heightened state of being gives you an edge, primes your body for danger and for reacting to said danger, so I allowed just enough magic to enter my system for my eyes to switch to Hidden mode. Allowing me to see where the hell I was going.

I followed a well-worn path through a sparse wood, past random picnic benches and a small play area for children that contained a zip line and other cool looking stuff I fancied a go on but resisted because I'm all about the job. Soon enough, the path led away from the direction Kate had told me to go and I headed cross country through the scrub, emerging in just a few minutes onto the boundary of an open, freshly plowed field.

The smell was strong. My guess was that manure had been spread earlier that day and the sweet, cloying mix of fertilizer and damp earth made me wonder how on earth Kate and Persimmon could distinguish anything else over such an intense assault on the old nasal cavities.

The land rose slightly, the view shortened, lit only by the moon and my own improved vision. Everything was washed out, gray and cold, like the world was covered in a fine layer of ash with all landmarks softened beneath a haze of truth revealed by Hidden sight.

With senses remaining on high alert I kept to the edge of the field, ignored the nettles and the hawthorn that snagged my suit, doing its best to reduce the already ruined material to little more than rags.

The hunger took me a few times as I walked, and I had to do all in my power to resist simply turning around, running hell-for-leather back to the car, and munching on my clandestine compadres. But I beat it by focusing my will, by remaining steadfast in my goal. Yet there was an understanding, almost an agreement made between me and the hunger within—come dawn, come the new day, and come the sun, it will be time to feast.

At the top of the rise, I looked down on what I'd least expected to discover. I'd imagined some spooky vampire stronghold, a large gothic building with an imposing gate and impressive grounds. Patrols, and dogs, and all the usual stuff I'm used to with the vampires.

Nope, none of that. Just what appeared to be a holiday park. The kind of place I would avoid like the plague if I was to go camping, although I'm not big on vacationing in fields as it plays hell with my suits and the showers are usually cold.

Amping up my Hidden sight I took in the layout of the place. A well-maintained road wiggled off into the distance then was lost behind hills. Probably joining one of the larger roads that would have a sign directing the holiday makers to their destination. One of those annoying signs that are half hidden in a bush and about an inch away from the turning so you have to drive for miles before you can find a place to turn around. And then there's no bloody sign on the other side of the road and you end up well annoyed before you even arrive.

There was a lodge at the entrance. Then there were other large buildings dotted about, probably leisure facilities, swimming pools, that type of thing. Maybe even a place for evening entertainment and overpriced drinks. And row after row of identical trailers, or what did they call them, mobile homes, static caravans? Something like that. Prefabricated oblongs that many people owned and used regularly throughout the year to escape the cities and get back to nature. Others rented out for a day or a few weeks to holidaymakers.

They were lined up at regular intervals over maybe five or six acres, and it was busy as all hell.

I took my time to get closer, but still maintained a very safe distance. It told me little, as the view from higher up the land was better, so I retreated, and watched the comings and goings for half an hour while I tried to figure out the best plan of attack.

It was impossible to know where Amber was being held, or if she was still here. Yet, somehow, I knew she was. Knew she was inside one of the buildings.

What did they want with her?

Guess I'd find out soon enough.

A Break In

Once I made it back to the car, I filled everyone in on what I'd found and suggested we go back to town and, more specifically, to Amber's. We dropped Persimmon at the alley and she picked up the bike then followed us to the strange, otherworldly place known as suburbia.

We had a few hours until dawn, but I still felt ridiculously conspicuous as we—a wizard, one in training, a necromancer, a vampire, and a shifter—walked casually up to Amber's front door and I used a little of the old magic to mess with the lock then flushed, grateful for the dark, when I remembered that it wasn't locked.

Inside, we retired to the living room and sat in silence for a while, just digesting the events so far and trying not to get overwhelmed by Amber's rather odd choice of home decor.

Mithnite was like a kid in a sweet shop. Unable to keep still, constantly asking questions about this or that.

Poor lad was more used to his old teacher's rather antiquated sense of interior design, heavy on the oak paneling and musty books, with a rather disturbing penchant for all things stuffed. And from the little he'd said of his life before his introduction to magic, I guessed his parents had been somewhat conservative to say the least.

Amber's place was like an Aladdin's cave of the bizarre. He stared in awe at lava lamps, sniffed at strange candles, and marveled at the rag rugs. Then he found the dope.

"Is this some kind of exotic spice? I've never smelled anything like it before. Is it oregano?"

We all exchanged a worried look, not because of what he'd found but because it showed how closeted his life had been. Poor lad really had to widen his life experience.

"No, dude, it's dope. Marijuana. Wacky backy. The stuff you use to make a joint to get high."

Mithnite lifted a large, fat bud up to eye level and licked it with the tip of his tongue. "Tastes nice. Can we smoke it?"

"Um, don't think that's a very good idea. The last thing we need is a Cheech and Chong style escapade with us running around on the hunt for munchies. Dancer and I already have the munchies bad enough and I don't think this will help."

"Aw, you guys are no fun."

"Look, tell you what. Once this is over, and it will be soon, I promise, we'll go do something cool.

Anything you want. But smoking dope is not a good idea for a wizard. You need to keep your wits about you and you need to stay firmly rooted in reality."

"But you said Amber was high when she got rid of the zombie virus. Most of it, anyway," he protested. He had a point.

"Different strokes for different folks, but now isn't the time." To change the subject I said, "So, if you could do anything at all, and it's on me, my treat, what would you like to do? What do you think you've missed out on the most?"

"Girls," he said without hesitation, then blushed.

"Girls. Hmm. Er, well, I can't really er... Um, I suppose we could go to a... No, that's not a good idea. Give you the wrong impression about the fairer sex. How about something else? You'll have to figure out how to meet nice girls on your own time."

"Well, there is one thing I've always wanted to do," he said sheepishly.

"Yeah, what?"

"I've always wanted to go to an amusement park. You know, where they have roller coasters and those rides that spin you around and the ones where you go down water slides in a boat shaped like a log."

"You got it," I said, pleased to have something, anything, to take my mind off what I knew had to be done.

"Cool, you all gonna come?" He looked around the room, eager as an imp in a lost and found, but everyone averted their gaze. "Come on, guys, it'll be great."

"Makes me feel sick," said Dancer.

"Makes me puke," said Persimmon.

"And I go green and then I fall over," said Kate.

"What, on a water slide?" he asked, looking at them suspiciously.

There were a lot of ums and ahs, so I said, "Okay, you lot, come on, give him a break. You'll come, won't you?" I met their gaze in turn, giving a slight nod, wanting them to give the poor lad something to look forward to. Heck, it might be fun.

They mumbled excuses but I said, "I'll buy you ice cream," and smiled my most winning of smiles.

"You need a shower," said Persimmon. "You too, Dancer. You guys stink of zombie grossness. Go get cleaned up."

"If you all agree to come to the amusement park," I said.

Once everyone agreed, reluctantly, Dancer and I left an excited Mithnite, already babbling away about how great it would be and asking if they could have hot dogs, and went upstairs to shower.

We found towels, but I resisted the urge to snoop. This was my daughter's house. I wanted to know every single thing about her, but knew this wasn't the way to go about things. We'd already invaded her privacy, her private space, by being here, and although we had her interests at heart, and yes, our own as well—zombie stuff, remember—it didn't mean we had the right to look at her private life unless invited.

And besides, the place had a very transient feel to it. Like she either didn't spend much time here or didn't expect to stay long. Just not like a proper home somehow.

Dancer waited in the hallway while I showered and wrapped myself in a towel, trying not to look too hard in the mirror as the infection had left my body a mess of discolored skin, not to mention the wounds from the events that preceded the bitey finale.

I got out quick and handed over the soap baton to Dancer who wasted no time cleaning himself up.

For a while we sat, wrapped just in towels, in the living room, both of us less than keen to put on our ruined clothes.

Silence descended while we all rested, everyone exhausted.

Everyone came and went in slow motion. Poking about in the kitchen, using the bathroom, trying to be unobtrusive and moving quietly as if the longer we stayed the more we felt like invaders. Rude, like thieves of privacy as we sat in someone's home and used what was theirs without invitation.

It was especially hard on Kate. Vampires can, and will, enter another person's home without an invite, but because of what they are it usually means only one thing: trouble. Vampires like to be invited in more from tradition than anything else, and this long-standing habit is so ingrained in the psyche it's almost like it's part of the vampire virus now. Part of the DNA they pass on to those they infect.

I battled to remain awake, so had to move. Standing in just my towel, knowing I had to get going and having finally come to a decision about how this should go down, I said, "I'm gonna go get dressed."

"Um, Faz, please don't freak out," said Kate, looking all kinds of concerned.

"Why would I freak out? And I was about to say the same thing to you as I have something to ask you. Actually, we may as well do this now, while we're all here."

"Okay, but, um, me first." Kate looked more nervous than a gremlin locked in an electrical store with fans of eighties movies, and I got a terrible sinking feeling about what she had to say. "Sit down, please."

I sat.

It was worse than I could have imagined.

Me, a Hippie?

"I found these for you and Dancer," she said, moving to a pile of clothes in the corner of the room and passing Dancer and I a bundle each.

"Huh? What are these for?"

"I can't stand the stink of either of you in your old clothes. You smell so bad. It's utterly gross."

"She's right, you guys stank something awful," agreed Persimmon.

"Yeah, like gross dead dudes," said Mithnite, agreeing with the ladies as he knew which was the winning side.

"Traitor," I said, glaring at him. He shrugged and smiled—not as daft as he acts.

"Kate, please tell me you haven't done something crazy?" I said, knowing this was bad. "You could have just stuck them in the washing machine or something." I glanced at the clothes on my lap then turned away before the full horror of the situation took hold.

"They were ripped and covered in nasty things, and besides, no way would anything short of a nuclear explosion ever get them clean. So, I got you those instead. I feel kinda bad for going through Amber's things, but she had some men's clothes so I guess there must have been, or still is, someone in her life. Go on, put them on."

"You're killing me here," I said, still hardly glancing at the "clothes" she'd provided.

"Go on, off you go. Give us a fashion show." Persimmon gave Dancer a special smile—they were definitely getting closer.

"Whatever," said Dancer, unconcerned by the fashion crime we were about to commit.

See, this is the difference between him and me. He wears black suits and white shirts because it means he never has to think about what to wear—I've never seen him in anything different. I wear retro suits and have lots of different shirts and ties because I like to look smart and because it's part of who I am.

This was almost sacrilegious. Scrap the almost, it was an insult to the clothing gods on an unprecedented scale.

"Fine, but don't expect me to like it."

We wandered off into the kitchen, Dancer with a lopsided grin because Persimmon was paying him attention again and kept looking at his torso and trying to peek under his towel, and I trailed behind feeling like a fool.

When we emerged a few minutes later, Dancer murmuring approval, me trying to hide behind him like a shy girl on a first date, we were greeted with blank stares.

"What? It's okay, is it? I was worried but you guys don't seem bothered." I stepped out from my hiding place and studied each of them in turn—nothing. Just flat stares as if I looked the same as always.

Then the smiles began. Then the guffaws, and pretty soon everyone was doubled over with laughter as tears streamed down their faces.

"I don't know what you're laughing at," I said moodily to Dancer. "You've got the same stuff on as me."

"Haha, yeah, but I don't care. You should have seen some of the things I used to wear way back when. This is all right. Nice and comfy," he said, lifting his arms, the kaftan with its long, hanging sleeves and laces that acted as buttons making him look like he was wearing a tepee. His trousers were a stupid design in bright green, with a saggy arse down to his knees. The legs tapered at the ankle as if he was auditioning for a Bobby Brown video.

"I care. That's it, I'm taking them off. I'd rather go naked than be seen dead in this stuff." I began to slip out of the "shirt" but Kate interrupted.

"Faz, come on, honey. We were just pulling your leg."

"Oh, gosh, wow. You mean you have proper clothes?" Please let it be so. Please.

"Um, no, I mean you look fine, just different. Right, everyone?"

They all began laughing again.

"That's it, no way am I wearing this crime disguised as cotton."

"You've got no choice. This is all that would fit." Kate stepped forward and looked me up and down. "Very, um, unusual. Unforgettable, that's the word for it. And the color suits you, brings out your eyes?"

"Yeah, and your tattoos," said Mithnite. "You look like a woodpecker that's fallen into a bottle of ink. Haha."

Like my life wasn't in enough disarray already. Now I had to go fight vampires and rescue my daughter dressed like someone who'd stepped out of the sixties and was into flower power, not the Mod look I so cherished. Amazing how the same era threw out so many utterly disparate fashions.

I took a personal moment and stared down at myself, trying to come to terms with the new look. I still wore my winklepickers, but that was about it as far as personal style went. On my legs were loose-fitting things some people apparently called trousers—as far as I was concerned if they didn't have a crease they didn't count as such. These were of a linen fabric in a faded orange, with drawstrings at the waist and ankles. Drawstrings! What was I, a bag for life?

In place of shirt, tie, and jacket, I was now festooned in a t-shirt from a psychedelic nightmare. Someone's idea of color on a bad acid trip. Yep, that's right, the worst tragedy ever to hit the catwalk. Tie-dye. A blue and white, baggy, low-necked, tie-dye t-shirt.

Oh, the horror.

I was there when this "fashion" happened, and I've seen it re-emerge over the years, and in some people's minds it never went out of fashion. Wrong! It was never in fashion. It's like taking all that's wrong in a garment, deciding it's almost perfect, but then thinking, "Hey, I know how to make this cool-as-Hendrix t-shirt utterly ace. I'm gonna tie it up with string and dunk it in a bucket of water I've peed in." That's how they do it. Honest. And not normal pee, either. No, weird pee that stinks of asparagus, or the kind you get after not drinking enough water. Proper nasty wee just to ensure you stand out as a real individual.

"Nobody say another word," I ordered. "Is there any coffee? Damn, why haven't we had coffee? I need coffee." My voice was rising; I was becoming manic. I was losing it and although I may joke about the clothes now, truthfully it was nice to have some light relief and for everyone to be laughing and joking. I was stressed because of what I had to say, what I had to ask.

Okay, you got me. I hated the stupid clothes.

A Big Ask

The coffee made everything if not right with the world then a little better. Amazing what caffeine and the familiar ritual of sipping on a hot beverage can do to help things feel more normal.

If we'd been in another place, at a different time, it would have felt nice. Friends sitting around, idle chit-chat as the outside world slowly awoke from its slumber and the birds began their busy morning, chirping and singing, signaling a new day.

But nobody could relax. Nobody was at ease no matter the brave face we all presented. There was a lot at stake, maybe more so than ever. Dancer and I may have been freed of the true undead infection but what remained was even more deadly.

Why? Because if we couldn't eradicate the hunger we would spend the rest of our lives unable to function. The desire for flesh would consume us. There would be no mindless life of the zombie, just our extended magical lives. I had absolutely zero desire to live whilst lost to a madness that would undoubtedly be the end result of craving human flesh at all times, the only thing occupying my broken mind.

We were right back where we started. We would have to be put out of our misery, we both knew this. But the decision now became that much harder. Exactly when would it overwhelm us and make us lost to ourselves? At least with the virus running rampant through our systems the signs would be clear. We'd wake up dead and then it would be something sharp through the old gray matter and that would be the end of it. But this? Ugh, it would make it more difficult for everyone involved as there would be no specific cutoff point.

Waves of debilitating hunger swept over me as I drained my second cup of coffee. I would be looking at Kate and her beautiful face, and the next her features would dissolve and all I saw was blood flowing beneath her skin, her flesh stripped bare, her brain almost glowing with an intensity that hurt my eyes, the power and lure of it so strong. This was no mere illusion, no subtle trick of the mind. It felt real, was real. Magic-enhanced vision layered over regular sight, making it just as true an image as any other.

I fought it and won, battled it down and locked away the urges and the sickening cravings that threatened to drag me under and never let me surface again, but it got harder and I kept breaking out in sweats that put most fevers to shame. Dancer was the same. Our connection seemed to grow, the more alike we became. Two outsiders that had to stick together if they were to defeat the objecting meat we wished to consume.

It was time to act. Now or never.

"Okay, everyone. Listen up. I have a plan and I don't like it, but I think it's the best chance we have, so hear me out." The room fell silent, all eyes on me. Was I doing the right thing? I wasn't sure, but I had no other plan and in my head it made perfect sense.

"If this place they took Amber is a vampires only retreat then the best time to get her is now, this morning. They'll be sleeping. The older, stronger ones, at least. But, and this is a big but, we know there'll be plenty still awake, and plenty that are dangerous. This is all assuming it is a vampire stronghold, which seems likely. Right?"

"No way would vamps take Amber somewhere like that unless they ran it," said Kate. "They wouldn't risk her being seen, or heard, by Regulars."

"Exactly. So, if we all go in there stomping around, guns blazing, well, it's gonna get messy and ugly real quick. We can't risk Amber getting hurt, which she may well do. We need to be a little more subtle. Try to get in there without it being utter carnage. Not until we find out what the hell is happening. We don't even know why they took her."

"So what's the plan?" asked Dancer, slapping a hand over the other as it reached toward Persimmon.

"Kate and I go in alone. We take the bike and act like I'm her, you know..."

"Her portable food supply," suggested Persimmon.

"Exactly. Chances are slim that the guys who took her will recognize me. They took no notice of us. We head in there, at least get far enough in to see what's happening, then take it from there. Kate, if you don't want to come I understand, it's gonna be dangerous. I can go alone but I figured this might be the easiest way to do this without hurting more people than we need to. Hell, most of the vampires might have nothing to do with this and it's just a couple of nut jobs. Doubtful, but this gives them the benefit of the doubt."

"I'll come," said Kate, resolute.

"You sure?"

"Yup. It's your daughter. We have to get her, and we have to do it soon. You and Dancer are a mess, no way are you up for a fight without backup."

"You're all forgetting one thing," said Dancer, sitting up straight in his chair and giving his hand a hard stare as if daring it to try anything funny.

"What's that?" I asked warily.

"I'm the damn Head. I'm their boss. There'll be hell to pay if they hurt me. They wouldn't risk it."

"Dancer, come on, man. You know as well as I do that the vampires think nothing of the Hidden Council. They look after their own and they only answer to their own Head. Sure, maybe you could call Oskari, tell him what's been happening and that you want Amber back. But you can bet he'll find out who she is, and find out what's happened to us, before he even considers handing her over. And you think he's gonna waste an opportunity to see you dead or to have this kind of power over us? No way will he tell these locals to give us what we want. He'll see it as the perfect opportunity to advance his kind no matter how well you guys have been getting on."

"He's right, Dancer," said Kate. "I know him, and I know how they work. If they see a sign of weakness it'll be exploited. And anyway, we don't have time for any of this. Amber needs to be freed right now, not when Oskari feels like it. He may not even know about these vampires. Could be a group of independents and they might not listen to him anyway."

"Okay, fine. But be careful, and do not cause more trouble than you have to, Spark. You know that if this gets out of control I'm gonna have a hell of a lot of explaining to do to the Worldwide Council let alone the vampires. Tact, and keep the magic to a minimum."

"Oh, one more thing," I said with a smile.

"I knew there was more," said Dancer.

"Of course there is."

We talked through the rest of the plan, until I couldn't wait any longer. Kate and I got up, drained our coffee and nodded to each other.

Time to go.

A Ride

The only sunglasses in the house were a pair of round, blue tinted ones. As I sat on the bike and revved the engine—having pushed it away from Amber's so as not to disturb the neighbors—with Kate gripping me tight from her position behind me, all I could think was that Dennis Hopper in Easy Rider had a lot to answer for. I felt just like him, which once I thought about it, wasn't actually a bad thing. He's cool, he's calm, but wild when need be, and sure as hell doesn't stand for any nonsense. In the movies, anyway.

Sometimes, it's hard not to think of certain parts of my life like one long movie gone wrong. They start off with me feeling like the hero, but things always get muddled along the way until I'm never quite sure if I'm still the good guy or if I've crossed a line somewhere. Usually I have, but it's always with the best of intentions.

This was one of those instances. I felt terrible for getting Kate involved. This was certainly not her fault or anything she need be involved in. But looking at it honestly, and actually accepting that she loved and cared for me, and would want to help given the opportunity, I had asked for that help, and she'd been happy to give it.

That's what couples do, right? They look out for each other? This was the result of a job gone bad, and she'd been involved in that and now this. I hoped to hell the next one was something simple.

The thought brought a smile to my face. So, there was to be another job, then? I was truly back in the Hidden world and back being an enforcer. I examined my own feelings and motivations and knew I was sure this was the right thing to do. For me. And for Kate, too. This was who I was, what I was, and there was absolutely no point denying it any longer.

I lived for this stuff.

A true addict through and through.

"You ready?" I asked, turning to Kate.

She smiled, such a beautiful smile. "Let's go my big, bad biker dude."

"Cheeky sod." We roared away into the east, the sun rising over suburbia. I pictured us from behind, a silhouette with a fiery ball of orange ahead. Then I had to slam on the brakes as a kid wearing oversized headphones, riding a snazzy looking bicycle, darted across the road, utterly oblivious, and the effect was kinda ruined.

Back on track soon enough, we left the burbs behind and sailed through the sleepy town. Traffic was light as it was still a good while until rush hour, and I doubted the fading town had that much in the way of traffic, anyway. Seemed that jobs were thin on the ground and traffic would head in the opposite direction toward the larger cities. Us, we were heading to a nice little holiday park that housed a horde of vampires and one strange daughter.

The answer to my hunger, maybe the answer to a lot more, too.

I had a daughter. This would change my life forever.

A Vacation

"So, what's the plan?" asked Kate as we stretched our legs just a short distance from the holiday park.

"We ride up and see if we can get a cabin, or whatever they're called."

"They call them static caravans or static homes."

"Huh? All homes are static. Unless they're mobile, I guess."

"There you go then."

"That makes no sense," I countered. "I mean, I don't go calling our house a static cottage."

"No, but it's made of brick and stone, not cheap metal. Anyway, they're all designed to be moved on the back of a truck." Kate shrugged and we were both lost to strange musings about the world of caravaning and these odd trailers, long oblongs of sheet metal that the British are mad about. I guess it's what the rest of the world would call trailers, so this was like a trailer park of sorts, but used for holidays or to live in for part of the year.

"You sure about this, Kate?"

"Of course. You're right. If I'm here it will be easier if its vampires running the show. And even if it isn't, you'll still need backup."

"Thanks. I'm sorry. I don't understand any of this about Amber. She can't be mine, yet I know she is. Who'd have thought it, eh? A daughter."

"It's kind of nutty. So she's like my stepdaughter. Um, if we were married, anyway."

"Yeah, I guess she is. Mrs. Faz Pound, I like the sound of that." Before I knew what I was doing, or had time to think, I found myself kneeling. It wasn't how I'd pictured it, thinking I'd pop the question when we were out to dinner somewhere nice and both dressed up. Not me half zombie and wearing tie-dye and trousers secured with string, but there you go, there's no accounting for love.

At least it was spontaneous.

"Kate, will you do me the honor of being my wife? Will you marry me?" I felt a tightness in my chest and my guts churned. Damn I was more nervous than the time I fought G'osah the Demon Prince of a netherworld I to this day cannot pronounce or even think about without going slightly mad. And no, it did not go well.

I held her hand, my palms sweating, and looked up into her patient, adorable, wet eyes. "Hey, what you crying for?" I asked.

"Because I love you. Yes, I will marry you, Faz Pound. I will love you until the end of time and not get annoyed that my stepdaughter is older than me. She better be worth this, though," she warned. "And I want to go somewhere sunny on honeymoon. Somewhere expensive."

"You got it. Um, no ring. Damn!"

"Haha, get up you idiot. And as for a ring, that can wait until we get home. Come on, let's go celebrate by kicking some ass and rescuing a damsel in distress." Kate wiped her eyes and I got up, hugged her tight, but released her quickly as the animal instincts took over and her scent drove me to distraction, but not in a sexy way. In a "Yum, dinner," way, which wasn't quite as romantic.

"Let's do this thing."

We got on the bike and drove the short distance to the holiday park.

"I wonder if Dancer and Persimmon are getting it on?" Kate shouted from behind me.

I shivered at the thought. "Now I've got this horrible image in my head. Like the day wasn't bad enough already."

"You better get used to it. They're gonna be a couple, I just know it."

Hell, Dancer was smug at the best of times. If he formed a relationship with Persimmon he'd be walking around with that thing he liked to call a smile on his face permanently. Although, maybe it would mean he'd do something about his hair.

Thoughts of Dancer in casual dress faded as we turned the bend and passed a sign that read, Val's Vacation Lodges. Time to book in.

Checking In

I parked up outside a modern building clad in cedar and pushed on through the door, holding it for Kate. Inside were the usual displays with leaflets advertising local tourist attractions and the rest of the space was a store for all the usual things you want while away from home. You know, cheap ready-to-go barbecues, bats and balls, fishing nets, strange shoes made of rubber, and inflatables in the shape of ducks.

There were basic groceries and a number of fridges and freezers stocking anything from burgers to fresh milk, everything overpriced as expected. What I hadn't expected was for it to all seem so normal. If this was a vamp den, you'd think they'd do what they could to make it seem less welcoming than it was. Hell, I already wanted to check in—it seemed nice.

Behind the counter was a weary looking woman of indeterminate age. Maybe late forties or early fifties, it was hard to tell. She had long gray hair, wore a thick, woolen cream sweater two sizes too large for her scrawny frame, and her face was so darkly tanned and wrinkled she looked like a walnut. She also looked utterly unlike a vampire.

Yes, vampires come in all shapes and sizes, but most prefer to keep youthful and fit looking unless they are truly old, and then they can't stand the sunlight. So, either this was just a nice lady working in the place, or maybe Val herself, or a relatively young vampire that didn't go in for outward appearances.

"Hi, you two looking for somewhere to stay? We don't get many people coming to book in this early. Usually just guests popping in for a pint of milk."

The woman eyed my clothes then kind of zoned out, maybe remembering times past. "Sorry. Did we need to book in advance?"

"Oh, no, we have a few statics left."

"Statics?"

"Yes, static homes. This your first time, love?" She looked at us like we were a little dense, and I suddenly felt rather awkward, hoping she didn't ask questions about the lack of helmets or leathers, let alone why we were here at all.

"Sure. We thought it would be a nice change. So, we can take a er, static?"

"Course you can. Oh, where are my manners? I'm Val. This is my place. It's nice and clean, no noise after ten, and you can barbecue if you want."

"Sounds great," said Kate. "You busy? I'm surprised you have room for us this time of the year."

"Oh, you know how it is, my dear. One whiff of rain and people would rather go abroad. We do okay, but usually we have a few statics available for people who don't book."

"Sounds perfect," I said.

A few minutes later we were the proud owners of a static home for the two-night minimum and down more money than most pay for their mortgage.

"Don't go thinking you can count this as a honeymoon," whispered Kate as we left and got on the bike.

"Wouldn't dream of it. Come on, let's go."

I went to turn on the engine but Val came rushing out the door and put up her hand. "Do you mind pushing it? It's very early for such a noisy machine."

"Sure, sorry. I didn't think. Don't want to disturb the other guests."

"You two traveling light are you?" asked Val, noting the lack of luggage and not even a helmet between us.

"We thought it would be fun. Spur of the moment type of thing. We don't live far away and just hopped on as we're early birds and here we are." Kate gave Val a nice wide smile and before she could ask any more questions we pushed the bike down the road toward our temporary new home.

We saw nobody on the way. All the static homes had curtains drawn and it seemed nobody was even up yet. Fair enough, it was just after dawn and pretty cold. As we approached our place I saw a man wandering between buildings, heading toward the main store, but he didn't even glance our way and was gone in a moment. It all seemed utterly normal. A typical holiday resort, same as you see all over the country.

Inside our oblong metal box, we sat on a tiny sofa, a cramped table taking most of the room.

"So, what do you think?" I asked Kate.

"I think Val seemed perfectly fine. She's not a vampire, if that's what you mean. Just a woman."

"That's what I figured. This place seems so ordinary. Think she's hiding something? Think she knows?"

"She knows, all right," said Kate, confident.

"What makes you think that?"

"The way she stared at your tattoos."

"Damn, I hadn't even thought about the ink. I thought she was staring at the clothes. She got this wistful look in her eyes."

"It wasn't the clothes. She knew what they were, what they meant."

"So Val is no ordinary middle-aged woman, we agree on that. Next step is to find out what this place really is and get Amber."

"We should do it now. If Val's in on this, or running the show, then you can bet everyone's gonna know about us pretty soon."

"Not just a pretty face, Mrs. Pound," I said, smiling.

"Hey, we're not married yet and it... What the hell are you doing!?" Kate smacked me in the forehead with an open palm and my neck cracked as I got some serious whiplash. The back of my head bounced off the window. I had the sense to stop trying to bite her arm again.

"Ugh, sorry. You could've just said something. No need for violence. I'm delicate."

Kate sighed and eased out of the weird seating area. "Come on, let's get this over with. The sooner the better."

I rubbed at my head—front and back—then squirmed and wriggled my way out of the seating-cum-eating area.

"Um, Faz?" said Kate from the open door.

"Yeah?"

"I think Val may have already spread the word."

I stepped up to Kate and peered out the door. There were about forty men and women in various states of dress all standing outside, all of them looking pissed off. "I think you may be right."

It was right about now I saw the flaw in our plan.

Things Get Weird

"Are you him?" asked a man wearing a blue bathrobe and pink fluffy slippers that may or may not have been his wife's.

"Depends on who you mean by him. And it also depends on who's asking," I said, thinking it sounded rather good.

"He's the one," said a woman beside him wearing a matching robe and a pair of oversized men's slippers. They must have been in a real hurry.

"How do you know?" I asked suspiciously.

"Because she said you thought you were funny. And the tattoos, and the vampire girlfriend."

"I'll have you know," I said, straightening my back and moving to adjust my tie, realizing I still had the stupid t-shirt on and was probably making less than as impressive an impression as I'd hoped, "she's my fiancee."

"Congratulations," said the woman. There were murmurs of the same from the amassed crowd.

Kate and I exchanged confused glances. Wayward dens of vampires aren't usually big on such things, and it put us completely off-balance.

"What can we do for you?" I asked.

"We want your heart," said the man with the pink slippers, who I wrongly assumed was the leader.

"I'm using it," I said, keeping my composure. Wondering how the hell we'd get out of this.

"It's special. We want it."

"Who are you people? What are you talking about? And where's Amber? If you've hurt her, I'll personally make sure you die slowly and painfully. And there'll be no chance of a— "

"Shut up," whispered Kate, nudging me hard in the ribs.

"What? I was gonna give them a good line. Show them who they're messing with."

"They already know," said Kate, nodding at several new arrivals. "The vampires are here, and I know who these people are."

Everything clicked into place. We were at a bloody Turning. Kate might get out of this relatively unscathed, if she was very lucky, but no way in hell would I.

The people parted as Val and a tall man with a cane, wearing dark wraparound glasses and a long black coat that almost trailed the ground moved forward, followed closely by half a dozen goons wearing dark suits but without the need to cover up or the weakness the daylight was clearly inflicting on the old dude. No prizes for guessing who was in charge.

The crowd stared at them all in awe, and no wonder. A "Turning Place," is a fancy name for what boils down to paying a lot of money to be turned into a vampire. They are always well off the beaten track, never advertised or discussed anywhere near anyone that could report the vampires to their Ward Heads or country Heads, and are absolutely not allowed.

They are also one of the main ways the vampires can run their own affairs so well—they are incredibly rich because of these actions. People in my position know all about it, but most Hidden believe the rumors that it is entirely off limits. Most vampires, too.

Every vampire is ordered never to turn anyone merely for money, and if they do and are found out they pay the ultimate price—death by imaginative, nasty, and painful ways. It stops the virus spreading until it's out of control, as any sensible vampire understands there's a fine balance between hunter and prey.

Let the vampire curse loose on the world at large and pretty soon there'd be nowhere near enough humans left for them to survive and flourish. They'd cause their own downfall and risk utter annihilation as no way would it be kept a secret from Regulars once the numbers reached breakpoint.

The truth is, all the major players were involved in this. The big bosses choose their people carefully, keep such business between those they can trust implicitly, or as much as any vampire trusts another, anyway. They give the select few, those that are told of their existence and believe, or are shown proof and then have to believe, the opportunity to be turned, if they can pay. Usually it's small scale, one on one, or maybe a few people over several days at a secret location, but that's just the Heads and the higher-ups organizing it properly.

There are still plenty of other vampires willing to risk all for some serious cash, and that's without the endless vampires unconnected to the main Wards or unassociated with any group.

No guesses for who these lot were. So, I believed.

Lone vamps, outside of the Law imposed by Oskari. Independent, and more than happy to turn a group of humans if they could pay the price and keep what they knew secret. Val's was the perfect spot for such activity. Remote, quiet, easy access, and great cover. My guess was that for most of the year it ran as a normal vacation spot, but was strangely booked up for a few weeks each year when the vampires-to-be came with their bloated bank balances, eager to get a taste of the promised immortality.

We were screwed.

An Invitation

"The infamous Faz Pound," wheezed the old guy, leaning heavily on a cane with a silver ram's head. Damn, but he lacked imagination. Next thing he'd be going "Mwaah," and morphing into a bat.

"And let me guess, you're the Count. One, mwaah ha ha. Two, mwaah ha ha. Three, mwa—"

"Silence," shouted Dracula the grumpy. "I am Kalle and you are not in Cardiff now, wizard." He made wizard sound like an insult, and that just wasn't nice.

"Look, why don't you toddle off back to bed if you can make it, and we'll just collect Amber and be on our way. If you're short of cash and want to turn this bunch of idiots then that's your business. I couldn't care less. But I will leave with Amber, so don't push me."

"Faz, be quiet," whispered Kate, although everyone could hear.

"Why? This guy's getting right on my nerves. He looks like he got his outfit from a joke shop, and I bet the coat's got a red lining and everything."

"He's Oskari's maker," said Kate.

"Oh, shit."

"Yes, oh, shit, indeed. You are most definitely in the wrong place at the right time, Black Spark. I know all about you and your exploits. And now it turns out you have a pretty little daughter. Come to save her, have you? I'm surprised it took so long. She's a tight-lipped one, but we know who you are."

"If you've hurt her..." Not much of a threat but they got the message.

"Fear not, my people recognized you when they picked her up. I was expecting you sooner. By all accounts you have a rather impulsive nature, so I'm surprised you waited until dawn."

"Oh, you know, kill 'em when they're weak and sleeping, that's my motto."

"Sorry to disappoint. I may be past my prime, but just like my dear Oskari, I am perfectly capable of being out during daylight hours. Just a little weak until I get going, but that's age for you. It comes to us all, no matter how we fight it."

I wondered how old this guy was. If he was a day walker like Oskari and looked this old, although now I didn't doubt he was strong, he must have been ancient. Thousands of years at least. His presence also meant it was very likely that Oskari had sanctioned this. Meaning, if I got nasty with him I'd put serious strain on the relationship between vampires and the Council. More specifically, Dancer. I didn't even want to think how it would affect Kate and I, and there was Mithnite to consider, too. Damn but families make things complicated.

The crowd had closed in around not only Kalle but on the trailer Kate and I had conveniently trapped ourselves in.

I figured now was about time to do the whole "grab the hostage and run away quickly" thing, so, without further ado, I called to the Empty and my eyes snapped to... nothing.

Confusion clouded my mind for a moment as Kate stared, wondering why I wasn't right now ripping through the vampire hopefuls or blasting away with the dark arts. Her having had the go-ahead to deal with anyone who interfered, and to hell with what Oskari thought. This was his problem if he sanctioned such things, but then I was lost to a different kind of need, an unholy want.

"Food," I croaked, and my world went black.

I stumbled from the top step, my mind restored like I'd blanked out just for a moment as something snapped in my head and the zombie hunger became not just a terrible craving but an absolute necessity.

Mind corrupted, body amped for magical interference, my call to the Empty was answered whether I wanted it to be or not. My eyes snapped to a black so cold and hard that my new desires rejoiced in the power it controlled to fulfill its need.

I screamed but it was no use. I was neither wizard nor zombie, not an enforcer or a father or a lover or a kind man. Hardly a man at all.

I was a beast.
The beast had to feed.

Yummy

All I could think as I tore through the terrified Regulars who had believed they would soon become immortal after surrendering all their worldly goods was at least the tie-dye looked better. Red always suits me and hides the goop, but this time the goop was very much in evidence, staining the shirt a dark, dirty red as I went berserk.

Kalle remained elusive, surrounded by his goons, but there was plenty of fresh meat for the taking. I was lost to myself, no longer in control. The virus gripped me tight and refused to release me until it had its fill.

As I scratched, ripped, cracked, and shredded flesh, bone, gristle, and brains, I suddenly got a profound insight. This was not only what it was like to be true zombie, but also vampire. When the bloodlust was upon them, when they had not fed for a while, they too became lost to the person inside. Unable to control urges that debased them, that controlled them.

Nothing could stop me short of death, and in my state that was highly unlikely. For I was me, Faz, but also this thing, tearing at flesh and cracking heads against any available surface. If it wasn't for the fact vampires were constantly on me, trying to take me down, then I knew I'd have had my first real taste of brain, so there was at least that to be grateful for.

I blasted the Regulars, maiming, killing, and generally acting wild, but something was still there inside with a degree of restraint, and those that backed off or ran away were left alone. I only attacked those that attacked me, so no sleep lost there. The vampires kept Kalle protected, the rest came for me, and Kate.

I watched as two guys, big and confident, did the vampire shimmer shuffle and were at Kate's side in a flash. I panicked and let magic swell my ink until the forces became almost unbearable and I was ready to blast them to pieces. But Kate was already away from them, her ability and speed far surpassing theirs. She was one hell of a sexy vampire, and she smiled at me as she circled behind them before they figured out where she was.

She slammed one guy so hard into a trailer that his head went right through the metal. He was stuck. He wailed as he tried to pull out but the jagged metal cut his neck to shreds. He tore at it with bloody hands, eventually peeling back the paneling. Hardly looking human, he slumped to the ground, head and neck in tatters. Moments later he was recovering.

A blur was all I saw even with magic-enhanced vision, then the guy was gone. Sailing through the air and landing twenty feet away. Bones broken and body mangled as he crunched into another trailer at the junction between wall and roof then slid down onto the grass, burning orange and shining with a pure intensity as the sun rose over the hills to the east.

More hopefuls attacked, but it was merely frustration rather than with any real force. They knew they were no match for the likes of me, let alone a me that wanted to eat them alive. Still overwhelmed by the hunger, I plowed through them with the taste of their blood on my lips, their scent clogging my nostrils, making it hard to think straight and consider what I was doing.

They toppled like dominoes, cast aside with impunity, little hope for those that refused to back down. There was no mercy, no room in my head for compassion. I neither thought about why they craved the life of the vampire nor cared. I was hunger imbued with dangerous magic, a Molotov cocktail ready to explode any moment.

Close to the edge, ready to erupt.

And then it passed as suddenly as it had come upon me. The hunger dissipated and I was Black Spark, deep in the clutches of my mistress, no less dangerous now I had the chance to consider my actions.

The crowd dispersed, those that could. They didn't sign up for this, would have believed themselves safe from outside influence at such a location. The wounded were dragged off, others left where they were. Some dying, some very dead, some being rather dramatic if you ask me.

But the vampires, that was a different story entirely.

"I just want the girl," I said, Kate and I holding hands now, standing amid the carnage and staring directly at Kalle, his retinue surrounding him, waiting for orders.

"You cannot have her. She's ours. Mine. She owes me."

"What the hell are you talking about? She's my blood, that makes her mine, not yours."

"Ah, the familial bonds. Tell me, Spark, how does being a father suit you?"

His words slowly sank in, and then I realized something. He'd already said he knew she was my daughter. How? Had Amber told him? "Why do you want her?"

"You know nothing about her, do you? That is to be expected. You absentee fathers, all the same. Think you can just turn up after endless years and take control. It doesn't work like that, Spark. You lost your parental rights a long time ago." Kalle had a sly grin on his face, that smug look people get when they have knowledge you don't. Condescending, and the kind of face you want to smack right into next week.

"Whatever you know, know this. If you do not hand her over, and I mean right now, I will destroy you, all of you. I don't care what Oskari thinks. I don't care what anyone thinks. I will obliterate all of you and nothing will stop me. If you know so much about me then you know what I'm capable of, what I am now. This isn't a joke, Kalle. I want Amber, and I'm out of patience."

Kalle Fossey leaned heavily on his cane as if gathering his strength, then stood tall, his frame straightening and his body coming to life. Guess it really does take a while to come round in the morning. His brow furrowed, skin thicker and healthier looking than minutes ago, and it became very clear he wasn't a man to mess with, day or night.

"How about this? You let us finish what we have planned and then I let you have Amber. For a while."

"And what exactly do you have planned? Why do you need her? What does she owe you?"

"She is to be my wife, of course." Kalle smiled a less than endearing smile and waited patiently for my shock to register.

I gave him no such satisfaction. Kept my features neutral. Kate gripped my hand tight, telling me to remain strong, and I think without that boost I would have just gone for it there and then, tried to kill Kalle and the rest of them.

"If she wants to marry you then I have no objections," I said, knowing that wasn't how this was working out.

"Don't test me!" Kalle's anger erupted, his face contorting as the mask faded, revealing his true, despicable inner nature. He was very different from

Oskari. This dude had no class, no sense of honor or pride in his conduct. An evil bastard in other words.

"No. The answer is no."

I should have kept quiet. Before the words were even out my mouth the vampires surrounded us and, knowing now wasn't the time to risk all our lives, I let magic fade as they closed in.

Surprise

I got a strange tingling at the base of my neck, a magical tickle that told me one thing. "Duck," I whispered to Kate and dragged her down to the ground. As I spread my body over hers, acting chivalrous although even as I did it I realized it would probably have been better for her to cover me as she's the fast-regenerating vampire and I'm the frail human, but at least I had manners.

Just in time, the world erupted with noise and mayhem as the trailer behind the amassed vampires exploded. Intense heat engulfed us. Metal, and lumps of plastic covered furniture flew in all directions. My shield was up just in time and boy was I glad it was.

Jumping up and pulling Kate up after me, I did a double-take at the fallen vampires. Those closest to the blast were pierced in multiple places by the metal, their clothes and hair burning. Faces grotesque masks of molten skin as they screamed and ran this way and that if able, batting at themselves to douse the flames.

Others were dead, the metal having penetrated their heads or hearts, no time to rejuvenate before their lives were lost.

The inner circle closest to Kalle had fragments of metal in their heads, but their bodies had been protected by the barrier of flesh behind them, and most were already pulling fragments from their skulls.

Kalle frowned as he yanked a shard of metal from behind his ear but I didn't hang around to try to deal with him or his followers. The Regulars that had backed off had fared better, well away from the blast radius, but they returned in larger numbers than before, everyone on the site now well and truly awake.

"Come on, let's go," I said as I pulled Kate off to the right where Mithnite was standing in the narrow road, smiling at us, arm still fizzing from the magic use that had exploded the gas bottles supplying the trailer.

He waved as we ran toward him, a cheeky grin on his face. Damn but he was getting good, if a little too proud of his own skills. A car pulled up to him just as we got to the road and Dancer jumped out the passenger side and ushered us all into the back to join Amber.

"Thanks," I said as he slammed the door shut then jumped back in front.

"You're welcome. Let's go."

Persimmon slammed her foot on the accelerator, crunched through gears, and we tore away before the vampires had chance to do much but feel the wrath of Faz Pound and his posse.

Good plans always rely on the unexpected, and I know vampires. The older they are, the cockier they get, and I knew that us being there would make those holding Amber feel confident and in control. They had acted as I knew they would, unable to resist the chance to gloat and to defeat me, never considering I'd use myself, and Kate, as mere decoys.

"You okay?" I asked Amber. She looked well enough, if a little shaken, but that was hardly surprising.

"Fine. Thanks."

"Did you have any problems?" I asked Dancer.

He turned while Persimmon focused on driving and said, "Nope. Just a couple of goons holding her in the last trailer. Easy peasy."

"Oi, you didn't do anything," said Persimmon, taking one hand off the steering wheel so she could punch Dancer on the arm.

"Hey, I kept lookout. And came up with the plan."

"No you didn't. It was my plan," I said, rather put out.

"I think it was all down to me," said Mithnite, trying to get more leg room, sandwiched as he was between me and Kate.

"All you did was a little blast. I had to go in and deal with the goons," said Persimmon.

"Yeah, but I finished them off when they ran out screaming," said Dancer.

I began to hum quietly to myself.

See, this is why I work alone. Why can't anyone ever be bloody quiet? I smiled at Amber and mouthed a silent, "Okay?" holding her gaze, looking deep inside her to find the truth of how she felt.

She nodded. A tear fell.

Mine, not hers.

A Long Journey

"Hey, it's not that way," said Amber, leaning forward in her seat, pointing to the turnoff.

"It is," said Persimmon, tight-lipped and clearly in need of sleep as much as the rest of us.

"We can't go back to yours," I said, wondering how long I could resist asking the million questions that swam around my head.

"But we beat them. You beat them," said Amber.

"For now. But they'll be after you. After us all. Kalle said you were to be his wife. That means he already thinks of you as his own. He won't give you up so easily."

"Where are we headed, then?" she asked.

"Cardiff," said Dancer from the front. "And we aren't stopping until we get there." Dancer coughed then made a strange gargling sound, a cross between puking and his guts being torn out his mouth. He cramped forward, moaned deeply, then shot upright and lurched to his right and grabbed Persimmon around the neck, pulling her head down. His mouth opened and his eyes were unfocused, the hunger utterly in control.

I did the only thing I could think of in the cramped stolen car Amber's neighbors would be right about now calling in. I punched him on the nose. Cartilage cracked as my exhausted fist connected.

His head slammed back and hit the side window as Persimmon shouted, "What the fuck?" then swerved to avoid hitting a tree.

We skidded across the road and stopped as her foot slammed on to the brakes, everyone flying forward, saved only because we were squashed in like sardines in a can.

Dancer was at her in a moment, clawing at her body, grabbing hair. I jumped out and ripped open his door, nodding to Persimmon. She pushed the seatbelt release and I yanked Dancer out and dragged him kicking, screaming, and thrashing into the side verge.

It was coming for me now, too. I felt the hunger rise like a sick emptiness that had to be satiated no matter the cost, and as everyone clambered out, shouting and screaming, I croaked, "Can you do this now? Can you take it away? I'm sorry, but it's getting worse. We'll be lost to it soon."

I hated myself for asking, for putting so much on her so soon after what she'd been through, but there was no choice. If this was to be done it had to be now.

Then I was gone. Watching from outside my body as I dropped Dancer and lunged for Kate, drawn to her because in my mind she was the tastiest, most delectable meal I would ever have.

I wanted her. Now.

Before I blacked out, I saw her fist come at the side of my head with all the power of the vampire behind it.

Which was nice of her, given the circumstances.

Ooh

Coming around tied to various objects was becoming a habit. This time, I happened to be bound to a tree, Dancer beside me. Frayed blue rope that stank of oil and mold was wrapped tight around our bodies, our arms pinned by our sides. Through the fog of my mind I understood I was back to myself because Amber was right this moment drawing out the last of the zombie infection. The hunger was fighting her, had no wish to leave such hosts, but when Amber called, magic came.

I didn't even try to release my bonds—no point freaking everyone out when I was quite happy where I was, thank you very much. The less I struggled, the sooner this would be over with.

Slowly, everything came into focus. Kate, Mithnite, Amber, and Persimmon were spread out in front of us, Amber looking like she was ready to keel over. Everyone else looked with concern from me to Dancer to Amber, not quite knowing who would collapse or scream first.

Dancer was mumbling beside me, something about brains, but I was past that now. As Amber's chest expanded, so bitter pills of diseased magic spat from my mouth like I was one of those kids' toys where you press a button and a sweet pops out the head. I was glad to be rid of it, and with each painful lump that scratched and ripped at my throat as it was purged, I felt a little stronger, a little more myself. A littler wilder.

Pure magic rejoiced at the freedom, at the chance to swirl and dance through my body. Channeled by my ink until it could contain itself no longer and I felt the tired scraps of the zombie virus leave my body. I felt hollow yet full, cold yet warm, sad yet ecstatic. Emotions and feelings all mixed up, most of me knowing I was back to being whole, a part of me still craving the blissful ignorance and freedom from feeling or caring that the infection had brought and would deliver in ever-increasing amounts if I'd just have accepted it.

Dancer spasmed, retched and coughed as Amber continued to breathe deep and suck out the poison. He spat and swore, still not himself, and Amber faltered, purging tainted magic she consumed to save us. Up it went, tarnished energy cleansed by her abilities, but still some of it taking hold. She battled and raged and swore as the terrible price was paid for taking such corrupt magic in such large doses.

When I draw magic from Hidden, I take on some of their sense of self, their very essence for a while, and such insights into the minds of others is seldom welcome. However quickly you send it on its way back to the Empty, vestiges of it linger for a while. Leaving you disconnected from your own reality, unsure of your own mind and emotions. It's a dangerous game to play.

Amber was clearly an accomplished witch, no doubt, but she'd been through a very stressful time. The fact she'd already helped us out and was doing so again was more than I believed I could have handled without having to wait a week or two to recover. At least the old me would have.

Something snapped in my head, like when a bone clicks and pain vanishes and you have full mobility in an arm that has been hurting you for so long you had accepted it as part of yourself. I felt utterly devoid of any foreign magic, anything corrupt. I was pure and I was strong and I was connected to the Empty in ways I'd only glimpsed for fleeting moments.

Dancer gave a final cough and a wispy trail of brown magic like dirty steam wandered from his stretched mouth and was sucked down by Amber, only to be released an instant later as something white and pure.

Her work was done.

I nodded to Dancer and he smiled. An actual, genuine smile, and we both knew we were free.

With a shrug, I burned through the ropes with heat so well directed it didn't even touch our skin or clothes. We got to our feet and rushed over to Amber as she collapsed.

She was freezing cold, drenched in sweat. The dark veins that had bloated her body as she took on our infection slowly receded and trailed away even as she herself faded from consciousness.

"We need to go," said Persimmon, "right now. They'll be after us and you can bet they'll catch us unless we get the hell away from here and somewhere a little safer."

"Put her in the car," I said, grabbing under her arms. Mithnite took her legs and we bundled her inside.

As everyone piled in, Kate stopped me and took a long hard look into my eyes. "You back?"

"I'm back, baby, and feeling fine."

"Good." Kate kissed me then, and it made everything feel perfect for a second before Persimmon shouted and called me a nasty name. I smiled at Kate and we got in.

Next stop, Cardiff.

Home at Last

Much as I was concerned for Amber, worried about vampires, unsure of my own mental state, overwhelmed by the fact I had a daughter, and confused as all hell about how on earth she was here, I was asleep before Persimmon was in third gear as she sped off.

Maybe it was the relief that the zombie fiasco was finally over, or maybe it was relief we had Amber back and could hopefully make sense of it. Whatever it was, my body decided sleep and recuperation was more important than getting answers. So I slept and didn't wake until Kate nudged me. I jolted awake, my neck hurting from the position I'd been in.

There was something gross stuck to my chin, and as I wiped away the cold, wet goo I realized it was drool. Not helping my cool image, but I guess that had gone out the window once I wore the tie-dye. My clothes were crusty and stank, in fact the whole car did. The windows were open, letting in a familiar smell, but not enough to eliminate the terrible odors emanating from me and Kate, covered as we were in the goop of vampires and would-be-vampires.

"Man, you snore like a walrus," said Mithnite, shifting in the seat beside me, but unable to get away as we were so squished.

"Do not."

"Do, too."

I ignored him on principle as it's not the done thing to get into arguments with young uns when you're supposed to be their guardian and teacher, and instead I looked out the window at the familiar sights. The city proper was off a ways, only the skyline visible, and as I got my bearings Persimmon exited the main road and took several turns then parked up under a bridge on rough land the local dodgy builders used as an illegal tipping site.

"Why are we here?" I asked.

"I made a call. It's time to ditch the stolen car," said Dancer.

No sooner had he finished speaking than several of his fleet vehicles arrived and he got out and spoke to the goons. A minute later he beckoned us all over and they got in our car and drove off.

"I'll take Persimmon home. You guys go home, too."

"What? Um, this doesn't feel right. We can't split up now," I said, the words coming out before I knew what I was saying. Everyone stared, expecting me to sigh with relief only too happy to cut down on the numbers so I could get some peace. Heck, I surprised myself. Usually, I'd be itching to get home and be left alone, but for some reason it felt like an anticlimax, like it shouldn't end this way.

This wasn't over, we all knew that. Didn't everyone want to get to the bottom of the mystery? Uncover what was going on with Amber and the vampires? Let alone exactly how she was even alive. And let's not forget the vamps would be after us.

All of this and more went through my mind, but then I realized one very important thing I somehow seemed to have forgotten. People are always after us. One preternatural creature or another is usually out to harm one or other of us, so it wasn't exactly groundbreaking news.

"You feeling okay?" asked Dancer, shocked at my strange outburst. "You sure you're not still zombie?"

"I'm fine, just tired. Okay, guess it's time to go home. Thanks for all your help, Persimmon, you saved our lives."

"My pleasure, as long as you don't make a habit of it," she warned.

"We won't," said Dancer, obviously keen to have some alone time with Persimmon. "Spark, we'll talk later. Maybe tomorrow. I've got a lot to sort out. A new headquarters for one."

"Sure thing, Boss."

The goodbyes continued for several minutes, then we were in the car. I got a front seat, Kate drove, and Mithnite and Amber settled down in the back, everyone relieved to have leg room. Ah, new car smell, nothing like it after being cramped up in a dodgy motor definitely not built for so many people.

We remained silent as we made our way out of the city and into the country, this time heading into familiar territory.

Home.

Kate's phone rang and she said, "Can you get that?" and I picked it up and answered before I had chance to think whether or not it was a good idea or even register who was calling.

"You better be coming to see Grandma, Faz, or there'll be no more tea, or hugs for you."

"Um, hi, Grandma, how are you? Nice day, isn't it?"

"Don't get smart, Faz, I'll see you in five." She hung up.

"Did you hear that?" I asked Kate.

"What do you think? Everyone in Cardiff heard it. Don't worry, I'm going." Kate took a right and switched back onto the road into the city.

"How does she always know everything?" I pondered for the millionth time.

"Because she's Grandma," said Kate.

"She's scary," said Mithnite.

"Is this a good idea?" asked Amber, looking nervous in the rear.

"I guess Dancer told you about her?" I said, already knowing the answer.

"He did. But everyone knows about Grandma. She's more famous than you, Faz."

"And a lot more dangerous."

One thing you can always say about Grandma, she does like to stay well-informed, but I doubted even she had any idea about exactly who we were bringing to visit.

Wrong.

A Growing Family

"My great-granddaughter," shrieked Grandma as she flung the door open and ran down the garden path.

She's never done that for me. I always have to let myself in and go get her from the kitchen, or have a hug in the hall if I'm lucky.

Amber, bless her, didn't freak out, not even a little. She stood, motionless, arms by her side while Grandma hugged her and squeezed her and showed no sign of ever letting go.

Understanding she'd be there until the world ended and hell froze over unless she reciprocated, Amber slowly raised her arms. First, she patted Grandma, which just elicited a tut, then hugged her back, getting tighter and tighter and tighter until they were squeezing for all they were worth.

I began to worry they had some kind of weird arm lock disease. Yes, I know that isn't really a thing, but stranger, much stranger, things have happened.

Finally, the embrace was broken. Grandma held on to Amber's hands at arm's length and said, "Let me take a look at you." Grandma can be pretty intense at times, and this was no exception. She studied Amber with such focus I expected her to turn around and do a runner at any moment. But she didn't. She held Grandma's gaze and she hardly even flinched.

"You look just like her," said Grandma, as she turned to me and smiled. And nodded. Then she frowned and said, "You stupid boy. How could you get turned into a zombie? Haven't I taught you better than that?"

"Hey, it's not like I did it on purpose. And I did save us all from being controlled by Dragon. Not that I've got any thanks for it."

Grandma waved it away. "I know all about that. And it was Delilah that dealt with him, or have I got that wrong?"

"No, Grandma. But we did our fair share."

"Yes. Dragging poor Kate and Mithnite here through all kinds of nonsense, silly boy."

"Grandma!" I was used to it; it's her way. She's often not big on showing too much emotion, especially in front of others, but this was different.

I realized something then, the reality of the situation sinking in. I think we all did, at about the same time.

"This is our family now. Wow, it's kinda grown pretty big pretty quickly."

"I'll have to buy more chairs soon," said Grandma. "Hello, Kate. Mithnite. So, you're my adopted great-grandson now, are you?"

"Um, kinda, Grandma. Spark and Kate said I can live with them, be part of the family. Er, if that's okay?"

"Of course it is, you stupid boy. Come here."

Before Mithnite knew what had hit him he got a Grandma special, too.

"Ah, what the hell," I said, and I grabbed Kate and Amber and then we were all hugging. A new family.

Yes, it was beyond merely dysfunctional and out the other side, but in this world you get few chances like this and I wasn't about to let it go no matter the questions I had. For that moment, wrapped in the embrace of my family, I let it all go. The hurt, the pain, the confusion, the questions I hoped I could accept the answers to from Amber, and everything else that was bad in the world. I let it go and clung to the moment like I clung to my family.

"Come on, you lot, inside. You'll have the neighbors talking."

It felt strange because it felt so normal. I'd walked into that house so many times over the years. But nearly every time I'd done so it was alone. Always me visiting the only family I'd known since a boy. Now I had a de-facto adopted son, a daughter, my wife-to-be, and Grandma.

It was gonna take some getting used to.

I didn't care.

I was happy.

Which meant something awful was bound to happen. That's just the way it goes for the Fazmeister.

Everyone Likes Tea

"I don't drink tea," said Amber.

The room fell silent, the bubbling pots somehow deafening as everyone held their breath. Grandma stared at Amber with completely blank features—she may as well have been saying, "Does not compute. Does not compute."

The silence stretched on and on until I had to nudge Amber gently to get her to see sense.

"Oh, er, I mean I don't usually drink tea, not unless it's a really special occasion. Yummy, smells delicious."

"Good girl," said Grandma, pouring the tea into Amber's cup. The best china was out and she even had a saucer. And, of course, everything was already set up for us.

Amber sipped politely and made appropriately happy sounds to which Grandma nodded knowingly—how could anyone not love her tea?

There were also sandwiches. Proper ones, with roughly cut bread, thin at one end, fat at the other.

"Take a sandwich," said Grandma.

"I'm not..." Amber took her cue from Mithnite nodding his head with great vigor. She took one and said, "Yum." Grandma smiled.

"Now, what have you all been up to?" Grandma knows most of what goes on, but the witch grapevine is not without its issues. Mostly in terms of downright exaggeration if not what they like to call, "A gentle manipulation of the truth for reasons of storytelling," and what everyone else calls, "Making stuff up as you have no clue but want to sound all clever."

"You heard about what went down with Dragon, or some of it, at least?" I asked.

"Of course. Nasty business. I told you to be careful of dragons."

"Yeah, but you didn't mention... Um, okay, so you know some of it. I'll fill you in on the rest another time. We got bitten and had to find someone who could help. And that's how Amber came into the equation. She'd gone to see Dancer, told him who she was, and he kept it a secret, until I was feeling myself again."

"Sensible lad," said Grandma.

"Lad? Okay, so, we went to meet Amber. Kate, Mithnite, and Persimmon came to help, even though they shouldn't have, and after a little bother with some vampires we got cured and here we are."

"I'm glad you're not a zombie, Faz, you don't suit green." Grandma got up to stir her potions and to be honest I felt a little lost. It's always hard to know what to tell Grandma as she knows I like to be independent and not worry her, but she also gets the wrong idea about events unless I go through the whole thing in painstaking detail. It would have to wait.

A thought came to me all of a sudden and although I was loath to ask I did, anyway. "Did you know about Amber?"

"Eh, what? Can't hear you." Grandma stirred pots so fast they splashed over the stove which steamed and hissed in ways you knew weren't hygienic. Then she turned up the ailing extractor, the clanging drowning out almost everything else.

I got up and carefully lowered the dial, trying not to breathe near the pots and wishing to hell she'd open the windows and doors.

"I said, did you know about Amber?"

"Only since she came to see Dancer," mumbled Grandma.

"How did you know?"

"I have my ways."

"Aha, so that's it. That's how you always know what's happening. You spy on the Heads, don't you? You have a way of getting in where nobody else can and listening in on what goes on. You never told me." It wasn't a question, just a statement of fact. I don't think I was even angry. Maybe it had been for the best.

"I wasn't sure it was the right thing to do. And no offense, Amber, but it could have been a lie."

"Don't be stupid, why would she lie?"

"Because that's what her kind do," said Grandma matter-of-factly. "They can't help it, not really."

I looked into the wise eyes of this little old lady. This woman I adore. The woman who saved me from myself, helped me grow into a man, and it lasted a lifetime. I saw such sorrow, such deep, bottomless sadness. But a strength, too, an inner fortitude I knew I could never match, never find it within myself to have.

Grandma would do anything to save me, to ensure I survived, and she would never risk me being hurt if she could help it. Not the usual beatings, battering, and near-misses I cope with on a daily basis, that comes with the job and we both know the score in that respect. No, on an emotional level where it really counts.

And this had almost broken her, I could tell. It tore at her heart to know I would be in pain, that I would hurt for a long time and she had played a part in it. Was the one to reveal the truth.

I smiled as the tears welled in her eyes, and with my heart so fucking heavy and my soul so twisted and raging at what was about to be taken from me after only just arriving, I said, "It's okay. I fell for it, but you know best. How long have you known?"

"Since the hug," said Grandma. "I'm sorry, Faz, I truly am. If there was a way to make this right I would have never let on, but you're in danger. I'm sorry."

"Faz? Grandma? What's going on?" asked Kate.

"Let's just go," I said. "Speak soon?" I asked Grandma.

"Very." She hugged me then, an embrace that told me all I needed to know. She loved me more than life itself and I her. Such a sadness we shared at that moment, but we had each other, and always would.

Grandma released me and turned back to her pots.

She didn't respond as a very confused looking Kate and Mithnite said goodbye, and a silent, eyes-downcast Amber all filed out in front of me.

"Just get in the car. I don't want to hear a word until we're at the cottage," I said.

Nobody dared to question me. Not those I loved, not those I hated with my very being.

I drove, just to keep focused. I refused to look in the rearview at Amber, held Kate's hand when I wasn't changing gear, and drove through my city.

It felt alien now. Like a betrayal of the joyous reunion and fresh life I'd anticipated less than an hour ago. Now it was a cold, cruel place.

A city full of broken dreams and shattered hopes. Mine just another in a long line of human suffering that endures through the ages.

Will this pain truly never end?

The Hardest Thing

"Kate, Mithnite, please go inside and close the door. Do not," I warned, "under any circumstances look out the window, come outside until I tell you to, or question me on this in any way. Do you understand me?"

"Yes, Spark, whatever you want," said Mithnite. Poor guy was utterly confused and twitchy as hell, and I wished I could tell him everything would be okay and I was sorry I was being so cold and distant. But I knew the words wouldn't come, that I would break if I even tried to be anything but just business.

"We'll see you soon?" asked Kate, absolutely terrified. She didn't know what was happening but knew it wasn't good. I'd never once shown her this side of my nature. Never spoken to her like that, and I prayed with what was left of my soul that I never would again.

I nodded, it was all I could do, and they trailed up the land to the house. Kate unlocked the door, looked back once, then they went inside. The door closed and with it my family. All that faced me now was a stranger.

What was to be a rant and a rage at the betrayal, the cruelest of deceits, focused violence and an end to this with as much pain as I could inflict, came out as nothing of the sort.

"Why?"

Amber shrugged her shoulders. No big deal.

That hurt more than anything else in the world, hurt me more than anything she could have said. She really didn't care that much at all. She'd had a plan and as far as she was concerned it might not have paid off as she'd hoped, but she'd got part of what she'd wanted and it was better than nothing. All of that was said in the simple shrug of her shoulders. Now it was over.

I felt sick. I felt empty. I felt like a fool. But mostly I felt sad. Not just for me—although there was plenty of that—but for her, for the race as a whole.

"You know," I said quietly, "I've met no end of cruel people and creatures in my time. Things you couldn't imagine, or maybe you could, but this is on another level. Just when I think people can't stoop any lower, can't hurt others in more inventive and terrible ways, along you come and prove me wrong."

"Just trying to stay alive," said Amber.

"And screw everyone else? If you wanted to get away from the vampires you could have asked for help. But this? This is warped."

"Kalle has owned me for years, wanted to marry me. You don't say no to that. I had to find a way to get away. You were it."

"And screw the consequences for me and mine?"

"Survival of the fittest," she said, her back straightening, saying the words with pride.

"We aren't in the fucking jungle. I'm a human being. I loved Sarah, I watched her die. I would have loved you, with all my heart. Given you anything in my power to give." A realization came, and I'd been blind to have not thought of it as soon as I knew the truth. "You've done this before, haven't you?"

"Lots of times," again with the shrug.

"If you shrug your shoulders one more time," I warned, getting right up in her face, jabbing my finger at her shoulder, spittle flying, "I will rip your arms right out their fucking sockets. Understand?"

She almost did it, but caught herself. "Yeah."

I was in hell, there was no other way to describe it. Utter, nightmarish hell.

"So, what, you wanted me to help you, get a cushy life for a while, so came to visit after you heard about Japan and found I was out of action?"

"Something like that."

"Bet the zombie thing was a bit of a shock, then?"

"Haha, you could say that. But it's easy enough to take others' magic. I just hammed it up a little for you guys to make it seem like it was tough. What can I tell you, Faz? I was in a bind."

"Don't call me Faz! Don't you dare. You don't get that right. My family, my close friends, only they call me that. You call me Spark. For now."

"For now?" asked Amber, confused.

I pointed at the spade, blade sunk in the ground next to fresh earth.

"Grab the spade and start digging," I ordered. A moment later I said, "Wait." Amber froze.

Something didn't make sense. This didn't ring true at all. Then it came to me, the real truth. Hell, just when my opinion of people was at its lowest and now I knew it was about to get worse.

"It was a trade, wasn't it?" Amber said nothing but had the grace to lower her head. "Yeah, you wanted to trap me, get me to that place as a trade. Me for your freedom. You did all of this to me, made me think you were my own flesh and blood, to free yourself?"

"So what? Everyone heard about you, what you did, about the giant and about Japan. The vampires talked about you, wanted your blood. But then you went and gave up magic. So I had to wait. I was so close. I called the vamps when you and Dancer were out of it at my place. It was perfect. And you ruined it."

I'd heard enough.

"Let me see."

Amber knew exactly what I meant, and her body morphed before my eyes. Her true identity revealed. She still looked a little like Sarah, just around the edges, but maybe that was just me, still unable to quite accept what had happened. She was a pretty woman, but her hair was dark, her features fuller, and her body a little smaller, almost elfin.

"I've met a few shifters like you over the years, shape-shifters, but never one so accomplished, and never one that had your skill with magic."

"Guess I'm just special."

"The things you could have done with your gifts. How you can take magic, your control."

"Spare me!" Amber's features creased in anger. "What, be like you? Spend my life chasing bad guys and taking their magic."

I'd heard enough, couldn't stand it for another minute. She'd done all this just to give me as an offering to the vampires in exchange for her freedom.

It was sick. Perverse. And she'd do it again and again, dupe people just to get what she wanted.

"Dig," I ordered.

Fresh Earth

Amber held my cold stare. Didn't protest, cry, or try to run off. She was resigned, and more than anything else I think that broke my heart the most. She wasn't surprised I was going to make her dig her own grave, was no more scared than any of us would be, or any braver. She just accepted it. To her, this was what people were like, how they behaved. This was what we did to each other.

I shut down my thoughts. Banished emotions, and watched with a dispassion and an emptiness that scared the hell out of me for it gave me a glimpse of my dark side, the true horror of what I am capable of.

Amber picked up the discarded shovel and the blade broke the rough turf.

"Not here, over there," I said, pointing closer to the trees. "I buried truly kind creatures here just days ago. You don't deserve to share their burial plot."

Without looking up, Amber wandered over to the trees, trailing the spade behind her, than asked, "Here?"

"Yeah, there."

She dug.

I stood and I watched a beautiful woman who I had believed to be my daughter, a piece of me, a piece of the woman I had loved and lost, watched die and mourned over for decades, dig her own grave. At this moment in time I felt nothing.

I couldn't allow myself to. If I let my barrier down even for a moment I would have been a broken man. Damaged beyond repair.

What was I doing? Letting myself fall for this kind of crap? I should know better. But maybe that was a good thing. I still had my humanity, still clung to hope and the belief good things can happen to people like me, people that aren't really good.

For I wasn't a good man, how could I be? Whatever Amber had done, I was making her dig her own grave and then I would kill her and I'd kick the dirt in her dead face and never think of her again.

Yeah, right, who was I kidding?

"Stop."

Amber paused her work and looked up at me with hope in her eyes. Hope that maybe she had a second chance, hope that she could leave and try again. Get a life away from vampires and away from me, be free.

What then, though? She was a manipulator, through and through. She would use others, use her gift and her appearance to break the hearts of innocents.

"Goddammit. Gimme the shovel."

Amber handed it over with relief.

It was short-lived.

"You saved me, but you killed me, too. Inside, you took too much. You gave me hope and you ripped it out of me. Too much."

She knew my mind was made up, and only flinched a little. Brave girl.

"What, you thought I'd protect you once it didn't go as planned with the vampires?"

"Worth a shot." Amber shrugged her shoulders.

I swung hard and fast with deadly accuracy. The sharp edge of the blade cut clean across her throat, slicing deep.

She fell into the long, weedy grass. She was dead.

I think I died then, too. Saved from the zombie virus, one kind of death, only to fall victim to another, much slower and more painful oblivion.

The loss of hope, of trust, maybe even of love. Certainly the ability to feel love without fearing the consequences somewhere down the line.

It was all stripped from me. I had nothing left to give.

Empty.

I fell to my knees and I wept. I don't know how long I remained there, but at some point I guess Kate and Mithnite came out and found me. Found us.

It didn't matter, nothing did.

Why is there always pain?

I'm sorry, I can't continue.

The End

Will there, won't there? Only one way to find out if this was Faz's last ever journal entry.

Subscribe to the mailing list and get notified of all future releases by Al K. Line—yeah, it's me writing this, but if Faz can talk about himself in third person, then why not me?

Stay jiggy,

Al

Printed in Great Britain
by Amazon

43531317R00154